# JOHNNY WAS
### & OTHER TALL TALES

# JOHNNY WAS

& OTHER TALL TALES

## GREG WHARTON

suspect thoughts press
www.suspectthoughtspress.com

Cover image and design by Shane Luitjens/Torquere Creative. Book design by Greg Wharton/Suspect Thoughts Press.


First Edition: September 2003
ISBN 0-9710846-3-8

Library of Congress Cataloging-in-Publication Data

Wharton, Greg, 1962-
  Johnny was : and other tall tales / Greg Wharton.
    p. cm.
  ISBN 0-9710846-6-1 (pbk.)
  1. Gay men—Fiction. 2. Erotic stories, American. I. Title.
PS3623.H37 J64 2003
813'.6—dc21
                                        2003010472


Suspect Thoughts Press
2215-R Market Street, PMB #544
San Francisco, CA 94114-1612
www.suspectthoughtspress.com

Suspect Thoughts Press is a terrible infant hell-bent to publish challenging, provocative, stimulating, and dangerous books by contemporary authors and poets exploring social, political, queer, and sexual themes.

Some of the stories included in this collection first appeared, or are scheduled to appear, in different versions, in the following (print and Web) magazines and anthologies: *Bad Boys, Best of Friction, Best Fetish Erotica, Best Gay Erotica 2004, Best S/M Erotica, Buttmen, Church-Wellesley Review, Exquisite Corpse, Friction 5, From Porn to Poetry 2, Homoeroticon, Judas Ezine, Kink, Love Under Foot, Men Amplified, Outsider Ink, Problem Child, Quickies 2, Roughed Up, Sex Buddies, spoonfed: amerika, Velvet Mafia, Venus or Vixen?,* and *View to a Thrill.*

To my honey, Ian,
my lover, my best friend,
and my muse.

# CONTENTS

## FOREWORD: WORD ENVY
## BY M. CHRISTIAN

I wish I could write as well as Greg Wharton. "No duh," I hear you saying—especially if you've cracked open this book or have been lucky enough to have read one of Greg's stories in print—"Who wouldn't?"

But it's different for me, you see, because I've had my share of moderate success—a story here or there, some books, that kind of thing—so this isn't one of those run-of-the-mill wannabe "I wish I could write like him" kind of things. Sure, it's nice to have been as lucky as I've been, but I'd trade it all to write as well as Greg. I envy him.

It's like this: I write, too—but when I write I become a storyteller, sticking my mitts up my characters and making them do this little dance, a waltz to dramatic structure, plot—that kind of thing.

But Greg, you see, he's different. Better, in my mind. Greg tells stories, too, but he does something much more important: Greg tells the truth.

I like to say that writers are liars, that it's our job to suspend a reader's disbelief, convince them that we're reporting what really happened, that what we're writing about is the truth, the whole truth, so help us...[insert deity]. That's what I do; that's what a lot of other writers do.

Greg Wharton may also be lying through his fucking teeth for all I know, but down deep, down around my heart, I don't think he is. Because Greg's prose, his stories, his exposition, his dialogue—everything that comes out of him, everything in this book, doesn't read like a lie, like he's making this stuff up. Everything here reads like the truth.

Pick a story at random, any one, and — for a moment — put aside the beautiful language, the playful descriptions, the lusty language, the wit, and all the other mechanics of writing and read. At the end you may smile, you may stare off into space while the layers of meaning, the lovely ballet of words, seeps in, but you will never, ever not think that what you've read is anything but the real, honest-to-goodness truth.

Greg tells stories but more importantly he reaches down into himself and pulls out something: maybe a part of his heart, a portion of his soul, a bit of his life — and writes with it. He might use words, but that's just the framework, the medium. The message is that here is life, truth, not fiction.

The characters in Greg's stories don't act like puppets or playthings, even though we might have fun with them and Greg certainly does, but rather these are people. They don't act the way we want them to, or expect them to, but like real people. They stumble, they dream, they hope — the way we all do. That's special. No, that's fucking incredible, that's what that is.

Beyond this ability to create characters that seem to live, breathe, love, and fuck, Greg is also just a Damned Fine Writer. If you read, and I presume you do or you wouldn't be reading this, then you know how rare being a Damned Fine Writer is. Some might be technically good, but lack soul. Others might be bursting with enthusiasm but write like a kid finger-paints: colorful but messy. Greg is neither, and that's what makes him and this book so great: he knows where to put each and every word, but as an artist, not as an engineer.

This might be considered by many people as just a "smut book" — one of those myriad porno-tomes on finer (and less fine) bookshelves anywhere. A lot of people, better writers than myself, have raved against the stigma of being considered "just" an erotica writer, but with this book Greg has shown us something more important than just labels. With his wonderful style, his proficiency and, most of all his way of writing that reveals truth, Greg has demonstrated that erotica is important not because the writing is excellent, which his is, but because the way he gives his stories truth and honesty shows us that sex is also life. The sex in this book is messy, weird, embarrassing, penetrating (in more than one way), funny, meaningful, deceptively simple, and complex—just like life. Also like life, in the hands of Greg Wharton the sex here is the best there is because it rings so damned true.

I consider Greg a true, good friend, and I think myself very lucky to know and love him. But beyond his smile, his brilliance, his wit, his brains, I really count myself lucky that he writes, and that he shares with us all the products of his incredible talent, his passion, his art, and the truth he gives everything he creates.

I just wish he wasn't so damned good at it. The bastard.

*M. Christian is the editor of over 12 anthologies, including* Best S/M Erotica, Love Under Foot *(with Greg Wharton),* Bad Boys *(with Paul Willis),* The Burning Pen, Guilty Pleasures, *and many others. He's also the author of four collections: the Lambda-nominated* Dirty Words *(gay erotica),* Speaking Parts *(lesbian erotica),* Filthy *(more gay erotica), and* The Bachelor Machine *(science fiction erotica). For more information, check out www.mchristian.com.*

## AUTHOR PREFACE:
## AKA FOREPLAY

This book is a work of fiction. Names, characters, places, and incidents are either products of the author's imagination or are used fictitiously. Any resemblance to actual events or locales or persons, living or dead, is entirely coincidental. Or is it?

A great author once wrote — and I paraphrase here since I'm a cheap bastard (er…I mean, poor writer…) and don't wish to pay for permission — that the function of the artist (and writing is art, is it not?) is to create what life doesn't. I've always appreciated this idea. It's lovely, romantic, and in many instances true.

But truth, real people, actual events and conversations can be stranger than any fiction. They can also be more beautiful. More amazing. More erotic. And more tragic. Our own actions, emotions, and memories, are more vivid than anything imagined. Painfully so, at times.

For desire can become so strong that it turns into obsession. Lust can make the wrong choice appear attractive. Love is felt not only mentally, but physically, and can consume. And a broken heart will not easily mend, if at all. These emotions are as deep as any physical wound and as long-lasting as a tattoo.

With all this in mind, I quite often use personal experiences, real people, and emotions of my own to guide my fiction, my own artist's offering of something that isn't already here.

Does this mean that all the characters contained herein are real? No. But a great many characters have parts of real people both known and not known — sometimes one and sometimes many within a single character. As a matter of fact (or were we discussing fiction?), some of these characters are a little crowded with all the real folk housed inside them. But like the perfect peach or apple tree, the flavors, textures, and scents of many varieties have been cut together to grow as one.

Have I had such heartache — as tragic a life full of pain and loss — as many of my antiheroes? No. Actually, I've had a pretty wonderful, happy life, full of love and many caring people. But I understand the dark emotions well, and for some reason that I know not, I tend to torment my characters with them more than many other authors.

I don't always have a clear idea where a story will take me once it has been started. I'm often surprised by the things a character chooses to say, or alarmed at the decisions they make. I can't say I channel these stories, but they do have a life of their own. I may be their creator, but I honestly have very little control over the journey that each will take.

Have I done all the delicious, wild, decadent, and sometimes depraved, sexual activity that my stories contain? I could say, yes...absolutely! How else could I describe it so you can believe it when read? And I could also tell you I've raped, pillaged, and murdered, like some of my characters have...

...No. Of course not!

An erotic writer — like any genre writer — should have a firm grasp of the material (s)he writes. And I do like to keep as firm a grip on my material as often as humanly possible. Sometimes, several times a day. Have I done most of the actual sex acts? Perhaps! I am queer and I do love sex. And some might even find my sexual activities kinky, perverted, or depraved. But, like the other actions my characters take, their desires, sexual appetites and preferences are their own, not mine.

My job as a writer—of short erotic tales, in this case—is to entertain, to take you on fantastic journeys with characters that will hopefully haunt you for a while. I hope I succeed. And though most of the stories contained in this tome are not classically structured "stroke" material, I do hope that they also excite you and, perhaps, ignite your desires.

Greg Wharton
while naked, San Francisco, 2003

## SWEPT AWAY

My mom used to love telling the story about how when I was a baby, a tornado swept into our tiny little Indiana town and took the roof off our house while we were in it. I was asleep and before my mom and dad could get to me it happened. The house shook, and then with a deafening roar the storm took off the roof just like the pull-top from a can of beer. Fearing I was gone with it, they ran into my room. But I was asleep in my crib. Slept through the whole damn thing undisturbed.

I got real tired of hearing this story when I was a kid, 'cause she told it to everyone. But now that she's gone, I like to think about it. Imagine me sleeping through something like a tornado. I can still hear her voice telling me...*but sweetie, you were asleep. The roof was gone, clean taken off, and your dad had pissed himself from fear. I was so afraid we'd lost you. But nothing woke you, not you, darlin'. You were safe in your crib, didn't even know anything'd happened. I don't know what I would have done if you'd been taken from me.*

I miss her so much. My memories of her are starting to fade, but the story stays with me. And the look of love in her eyes, all misting up, every time she told it. Her sad pretty brown eyes told it all. I remember her sad eyes the most.

So what did they do? My parents moved a hundred miles east to Ohio to another little town, where we get even more storms. But that's not what got mom. She got cancer. It ate her up from the inside and she died when I was still a little pup.

Forget the Big One. The earthquake that everyone always talks about ripping through California and separating it from the rest of us. Nothing could compare to a couple of funnel clouds coming down out of nowhere and flattening everything in their way. It happens. It happens so quick you don't have time to think, and it happened to us a couple years ago. I was at school. The alarms went off, but it was over before we knew it.

Three of them hit the town that day. I was fourteen. Not many folks died, just a few I didn't know in the trailer park where some of my school friends lived, but about half of us lost our homes. It made national news. It also killed my dad. Well, the storm didn't kill him, but losing his home almost did. Then he lost his job because the plant he worked in was flattened. Then the heart attack. You get the idea. Another year sitting at home doing nothing but drinking, then he was gone.

That's how I ended up living with my stepmom June. And I guess that's why I have such bad dreams about cyclones and all. At least, that's what my doctor says. Dr. Fogerty: my shrink. He says *You have acute separation anxiety over losing both parents and I suspect once you meet the right girl and fall in love the bad dreams will stop.* He doesn't do me much good, but I do enjoy writing in my journal. And I have a good stash of meds for the occasional party or concert with my best friend Pip.

Dr. Fogerty told me to write down my dreams. Keeping track of them would be good for me he said, so I started the journal. I don't even write in it every night. When I do, it's mostly about the dreams when they come, and how they make me feel.

June married my dad a year before the storms took our town. She's nice enough, pretty, and she loved dad so much. She told me she would always take care of me. And she has; though I'm almost as old as she was when she met my dad and I don't really need that much taking care of. But she loves me, feeds me every night before she starts her shift at the bar, and makes sure I get my homework done. She's my family now.

I just wish she would stop leaving the *Hustler*s lying around. She doesn't read them. They're for me. Last month she found my journal. It was the day after my first time with Jackson. The day after I finally found out how sweet his lips tasted, the day after I let him fuck me and I fell in love. I came home and wrote it all down, then crashed. I woke up late and had to rush to get to school on time.

I left the journal out on my bed. And she read it. Most of it I wouldn't mind her seeing. Most of it. But I was so excited when I got home that night; I had to write it all down.

Jackson and me had always got along okay, but he was a jock, on the football team. And I was, well, I'm just me. He and I were in a few classes together and he always said *hi* to me and stuff, but we never hung out. I've always thought he was hot. I'd even sneak into the locker room after his football practice to try and catch a glimpse of him undressing or in the shower.

I guess I should be honest. I've always liked guys. I know that's who I am. I just don't tell anyone. Except for my friend Pip. She knows everything about me.

I can tell her. We've been best friends since my folks and I moved here or just about. The first time I told her anything, we were skipping class and getting high in the woods behind her house. I just blurted it out. *I like guys, Pip. I have sex with them. I suck guys' dicks. Lots of dicks. And one day, I'm gonna find one that loves me and we're going to move in together. And I'll never be lonely.*

But that was before I had ever done anything. She knew it too, but didn't say so. When I finally did it with a guy, she was so happy for me she made me tell her all the details. And I did. Only it wasn't that exciting. Just some guy at Jolly's Diner who took me into the bathroom and sucked me off. It was quick and I never saw him again. I'm not sure his name really was Don. But it was a start.

One time, I was cutting through the locker rooms at school and saw that Jackson was still in there long after all the other guys had gone. He didn't see me, but I saw him. I saw all of him. I started to cut through on my way home every day, and sometimes he was there, the last to shower, alone. And I'd watch him.

So a couple weeks later, I cut through real quick as if I really do it to get home and he was sitting on one of the benches. He wasn't naked. He had his jeans on, but no shirt. He was wet. His hair was dripping and I just stopped dead in my tracks and watched him as drops of water fell down his smooth chest. There was a pool of water around his big wide feet and he was just kind of tapping around in it like he was dancing. I don't know, I must have looked like a deer caught in headlights, but he didn't freak out or hit me or anything. He just smiled real wide and said *Hey, Van, where you off to? Want to hang out?* He acted like we were best friends.

We went back to his house after he got dressed and drank some beers while sitting on an old couch in the basement rec room. Just hanging out. I asked him about Belinda, his girlfriend, and he says *Belinda's all right. I'm planning on going away to college after graduation though. So we're not that serious. You know chicks. Don't tell anyone, but she doesn't even let me do her that much anymore. Besides, I like to jerk off more, know what I mean? What do I need her for?* And he was rubbing himself through his jeans. He was hard and it was pushing up through the worn fabric. I could see every inch. Then he leaned over and kissed me.

His lips were just as I had imagined, all sweet and soft. Fireworks went off. I closed my eyes and bright white flashes exploded. My heart just about broke out of my chest as he pulled me to him and held me tight. I couldn't hardly breathe as he lay down on top of me. His tongue explored my mouth like he wanted to eat me, like he was hungry. And he rubbed himself hard against me. And I rubbed back as well as I could from underneath.

It wasn't like the guy at Jolly's who finished me

off in about two minutes then split. We took our time. He let me do everything I had always wanted to do. I put my hands and mouth and dick everywhere I'd always dreamed of. It was like he wanted me just as much as I wanted him.

My favorite part was the kissing. We would kiss — open and sloppy — and I would force my tongue deep into his mouth and he would moan and shake as if a force bigger than both of us was taking over.

I didn't tell him, but when he stuck it in me, I knew I was in love. And when he came, holding me tight and whispering *I like you so much, Van. You feel so good. I really like you. Damn...you feel...I love...*to the back of my neck, I cried tears.

And I wrote it all down. And June read it. I think the *Hustler*s are just her way to encourage a healthy lust for the female or something. She didn't yell at me. She didn't even say anything to me. But when I got home that afternoon, my bed was made and the journal was closed up and on my nightstand. And the first of many *Hustler*s was on the coffee table.

I think my dreams are just a way of me getting out the feelings that are inside me. They used to be of my mom and me floating arm in arm in the middle of the cyclone, then she would get pulled away from me and I wouldn't be able to see her anymore. She would be gone. I always woke up afraid and crying.

Since I've started doing it with Jackson, I haven't had but one bad dream. In it, we're walking hand in hand, barefoot through the sod farm out on Old Fort Road, when I see the familiar black funnel cloud. Only this time I'm not afraid. We just stop and watch it approach, pulling up everything in its path. Jackson says *Hold on to me, Van. Nothing can hurt you if you hold me tight. Don't be afraid.* And I do. And I'm not. But we still get pulled up into the center. I hold tight. I feel his strong arms around me as we twirl around and around, but he still leaves me. Floating away in the debris until I can no longer see him. Up and away and then gone.

I love Jackson. I love his big arms and hands and the way we fit together when we do it. I love watching him over me when we're all hot and heavy and the way his sweat snakes down and drips from his nipples onto me. I love his swagger and the way he looks from behind. I love the way his breath smells like menthol cigarettes, and the way his mouth always tastes a little like milk, and I love the funny way his hair grows all crazy on the top of his head since he has a double crown.

I love Jackson, but I'm sure that he's going to leave me. It's not just the dreams. But I know. I can feel it when we kiss now. It's different somehow. No fireworks. No bright white flashes.

I don't think he's going to get his football scholarship to college like he planned though. Maybe he'll stay here and marry Belinda and just have babies. Or something. I'll miss him I'm sure. I don't know—maybe he'll miss me. I sound pretty calm. I'm not. I know I'm never gonna find another that compares to him. That's just the way things happen for me.

Pip's busy with getting ready for college now and we don't talk as much. She's leaving soon. All the way to New York. June's got a new man and even though she wouldn't ever do anything to hurt me like throw me out, I know she's thinking of marriage again. She's in love, too. That's good. I guess I'll get my own place. It's time.

Maybe I should move. When Jackson finally does leave me, I could go to California and wait for the big one. At least there's no tornadoes to get swept away.

## BLOOD ORANGES AND COTTON CANDY

It's illegal to operate a cemetery in the city of San Francisco.

In the late 1800s, San Franciscans became increasingly concerned about the public health problems created by city cemeteries as well as about the ever-decreasing available space for the growing city. If you have ever visited San Francisco, you know that it is now packed about as tightly as any city you'll find. In 1902, the city's board of something voted to outlaw any more interments within the city limits. They also demanded that the largest cemeteries in the city move their bones elsewhere.

This created a problem. Obviously, San Francisco still had people dying, and they needed to be buried somewhere. Following the lead of the Catholic church and a certain Archbishop Patrick Riordan — who had begun in 1892 to bury their dead in an old potato field five miles south of San Francisco — many people began to look to the small city of Colma. Quickly, this town of about 1,200 people took on a character of its own. Over a million people are buried in the town of Colma, the only incorporated city in America where the dead outnumber the living.

My name's Paul. You can call me Tara. This is where I grew up.

My father — before he died — and his father — before he died — ran a funeral home. Not your fancy big homey high-end kind of funeral home. No, Jackson and Sons Funeral Home was what you might call your cut-rate no-frills funeral home. He died there, my father, of a heart attack. In the basement while trying to piece together some dead guy's head who had stepped in front of a MUNI bus.

When he died, my mom sold the business and our house to another family funeral home down the block. There's one just about every block. In some cities there's a Starbucks on every corner. In Colma, you get funeral homes. I didn't want anything to do with Jackson and Sons. Mom used the money to open a floral shop. It did well. As long as people keep dying, there'll always be a need for flowers in Colma.

I'm an only child. My younger sister died during birth. Her name was Mary. Is Mary. It would have been nice to have a sister, a live one that is. But Mary is still around. She visits in my dreams and shows me things. Not that most of them come true. Most don't. I'm glad they don't. It would be too spooky to have that gift, or rather have a dead sister who comes to you in dreams and shows you the future. Mary takes me for rides: some dark that let me see what might happen to those who hurt me, and some that are just fun. Adventures. My therapist knows about Mary but thinks she's really just dreams working out day-to-day stress. Maybe so, but I'm glad she's there.

Well, it isn't exactly true that I'm an only child. I do have a brother. His name is Peter. He's two years older than me. He's a conservative right-wing homophobic fucker, a headstone maker, who thinks I should have been the one to die during birth. I prefer to pretend he never happened, and succeed most of the time. We don't talk. Haven't since high school. Probably won't ever again. He's dying of cancer.

Needless to say, my teenage years were spent trying to get out of Colma. And the years since leaving have been spent trying to deal with the damage that leaving couldn't heal.

\*\*\*

*Mary and I float above the house we have always lived*

in. A house that is also a funeral home. I am 10 and she would be 8. Unlike our parents, and Peter and I, who have jet-black hair, Mary's hair is pale blond. It glows like bright light around her face. She is wearing a long white v-neck t-shirt that looks like it's one of my Dad's. She's so pretty. I love her.

"I'm so glad you're here, Mary," I tell her.

"I am too, Paul. I am too. I'm here. I'll always be here with you," she says. "Daddy is hurting, Paul."

"He is? I don't want Daddy to hurt."

"I know, Paul, but he'll be fine. He is going to die. It is his time. See…"

We watch my Daddy in the basement work area. A red glow comes from his heart, then his left arm. He grabs his arm then drops the long syringe he is holding. It bounces off the edge of the ceramic and metal table where he works on the bodies and falls to the floor with a clang. Daddy tries to move away from the table but just jerks, then quietly lays his body over the corpse he has been working on. We watch Daddy die.

"No!"

"It will be fine. Don't be sad. Sometimes it's just your time. Even if it's not fair. And I'll always be here with you no matter what happens."

***

"Green Tara is the loving goddess who is waiting to help you cross the ocean of Samsara, which is the illusory world perceived by the ego."

Jennifer is my best friend. We are seniors at Patrick Riordan Catholic High School. She is reading to me while I do her toenails. I am painting them a deep green to match her fingers, which we did earlier at her house. We ate some pot brownies that her mom, Sue, had made and then came down here to our favorite grave in Final Rest Cemetery to be high and smoke our clove cigarettes. Sue said pot was okay, but she wouldn't let Jennifer or her friends smoke cigarettes in the house — especially the clove ones we liked. Sue said they would give us a "urinary infection" if we weren't careful.

"Traditionally offering protection from drowning, thieves, lions, snakes, fire, spirits, imprisonment, and wild elephants — here, look how beautiful she is."

Jennifer hands the book down to me and I look at the detailed color drawing of the bald green goddess.

"Looks like you, Jen."

"Yeah, I know. Call me…Green Tara —" and she starts cackling madly. The pot from the brownie must have started to hit.

I hand the book back and giggle with her while I finish her toenails.

"Green Tara — that's me! — brings courage to see things in new ways and to move in new directions. Historically, Green Tara was the Nepalese princess who married Songsten Gampo, the first Buddhist King of Tibet. Hey, Paul! I was married to a King!"

I finish the last nail, the scary one on her little toe. It's tiny and gross, not more than a misshapen little strip about the size of an ant.

"Maybe I was King Gampo!" I exclaim rising to my feet and twirling around.

"No, listen. The same king also married a Chinese princess known as White Tara. That's you, Paul! White Tara!"

"Cool. White Tara and Green Tara. I likes!" I sit back down and take off my Doc Martins, then my socks, so I can do my own toenails.

Jennifer leans back against the gravestone and lights a cigarette. It sizzles every time she draws the heavy smoke into her lungs. She coughs and I look up. Her long straight hair — cut shoulder length, exactly the same as mine — has been bleached then dyed both blue and black. It glows an unnatural blue-black in the sunlight. Mine I've left its natural black.

"So here's our new chant, White Tara —"

"Yes, my Green Tara?" I ask as I finish foot number one and start on the second.

"OM TARE TUTTARE YE SWAHA—"

Sue's brownies kick ass. It must be the brownies. I don't understand what she is saying. I start laughing and fall over forgetting about the last couple of toes.

"OOM TARE TUTTARE YEEEEEEEEEE SWAHAAAAAAAA," she sings.

"You sound like Lisa Gerrard!"

"Kick ass! You know it! DEAAAAD CAN DAHHHHNCE! DEAAAAD CAN DAHHHHNCE! OOM TARE TUTTARE—"

"What's that for?"

"It's the suggested meditation for compassion and protection…"

I roll onto my back looking up at the blood orange tree that hangs over us. I see an orange that had dropped by my arm and I pick it up. It's overripe and covered in ants and it opens up when I touch it. Its juice rolls down my arm, warm and sticky, like blood.

"…relax your body and allow your mind to clear…"

***

*Mary and I float above Final Rest Cemetery. I am 14 and she would be 12. She is taller than me and her shiny white hair is long and blows in the wind. She is wearing one of my Mom's nightshirts and she has the sleeves rolled up because they are too long. She's eating a blood orange, slowly peeling off one section off at a time and putting them in her mouth.*

*"I missed you, Mary."*

*"I missed you too, Paul. But I've never been far away."*

*"Peter hurt me, Mary. He hurt me pretty bad."*

*"I know. But you will be fine. You'll see."*

*"It doesn't feel that way. His friend Jared —"*

*"I know, honey. I know. But you'll be fine. And he'll die soon enough."*

*"Jared?"*

*"No. Peter. Even now it grows. See…"*

*We look down and see our brother Peter jerking off in his room of the split two-level house that Mom and Peter and I live in. He is lying on his back on his bed, his thin long pale dick in hand. A red glow comes from his balls. He masturbates and comes in stringy globs onto his stomach, then takes a Kleenex, wipes it off, and tosses it across the room to a trash can.*

*"What — "*

*"Cancer. He'll start having great pain in a couple years, then he will die before he's thirty."*

*"That's good. He deserves it. But you won't leave me will you?"*

*"No, Paul. I'll always be with you no matter what happens."*

\*\*\*

I run as fast as I can, but it isn't fast enough. Two blocks with a head start get me to Final Rest Cemetery. But they catch me. My brother Peter and his best friend Jared catch me. They are royally pissed, and I am fucked.

My brother manages to trip me and I fall down, falling flat on my face nearly hitting my head on a gravestone. He pounces on me, sitting on my back and gripping my wrists above my head so they scrape against the stone.

"You are so fucked now you little faggot!" screams Jared as he catches up to us.

"It was a misunderstanding, Jared. Jesus, get off me! Come on, Peter, let me up!"

I am trying hard not to cry. That would surely give them even more reason to kick me around. I can taste blood in my mouth and my bottom lip is starting to swell. My brother's hands are gripping my wrists roughly and my hands are getting numb.

"Shut up, you little pussy!" Peter says. His anger scares me. It always scares me.

I start whimpering. "I'm sorry. Fuck, I'm sorry, Peter. Let me go. Please, I'm sorry."

My brother's weight lifts from my back, but his grip on my wrists grows firmer. Then he kneels on one of my arms and grips my hair with the now free arm. He lifts my head back and whispers in my ear, "Jared always said you were a faggot. Now we know the truth. I don't know what you thought you saw, but it was nothing. Nothing! You hear!"

I smell the wet earth. I smell the fresh sod, and mud, rotting oranges, and my blood. I smell the cement of the gravestone and the dying flowers right next to my white knuckles. I smell my brother's angry sweat and I smell my fear as I feel Jared's arms reach around under my stomach and unbutton my shorts.

My vision is blurred from my tears. I'm crying and my nose is running. It's too late to worry about being a baby. I try unsuccessfully to sniff the snot back into my nose as I cry out for them to stop…for them to stop…please no…Jared…don't…stop!

\*\*\*

I always get home from school before Peter. Mom works at her flower shop until six or so every night, so I usually come home, fix a sandwich, and do whatever homework I have to early — while the house is empty and silent.

I'm sitting in my room at my desk listening to the radio, trying to ignore the math I don't understand in front of me. I get up to look for my Culture Club cassette. But it's not there.

"Fucking Peter!"

I storm out of my room and down the hall to Peter's room, blaming him for taking my tape even though he hates Culture Club and probably didn't take it. I'm just mad at the math.

I stop once I'm inside his room and look around at the mess. I'm rarely inside his room since we're not exactly best friends. If my tape was in here I sure as hell wouldn't be able to find it. There are heaps of clothing everywhere. His bed looks like he hasn't changed the sheets in years and it kinda stinks bad. Like him. What a loser!

The front door slams and I panic. I hear him running up the steps and there's no time for me to run back down the hall. Fuck! I open one side of his sliding closet door and climb inside, kicking a pile of clothes out of the way. Crouching down, I pull it almost shut just as he and his ignorant friend Jared come in.

"Wonder where the fag is?" Peter growls.

"Out suckin' dick, no doubt," Jared says.

"Yeah, probably."

"He ever do you?"

"What? No way!" Peter squeaks. My brother's voice squeaks when he's excited.

"You ever do him?"

I'm so scared I'm shaking. Here I am trapped in my brother's lair. It's hot. It's stinky. And if he finds me I'm dead meat. Dead meat. I'm in the right town anyway. I fight back a giggle. I always laugh at the wrong things…and at the wrong times.

"Shut the fuck up!"

"Sorry, man. Settle down. I'm just horny. It's my hard dick talkin' that's all. You want to jerk off?"

"I told you that was a one time thing!"

What? My brother jerks off with Jared?

I peak my head out a little and I can't believe what I see. Jared has pulled his dick out and it's hard. He slides his pants down around his ankles and starts stroking his dick hard and fast. My brother is sitting on the bed right by him. Jared turns and puts his dick right in Peter's face.

"Come on, man, suck it."

And I lose my balance. I fall out of the closet nearly ripping the sliding door off. I land with a thud right at Jared's feet with a "Shit!" from both me and him.

I've never been a runner, but I give it all I have. I run. I run from Peter's room and I run from my house. And I run from his anger. Peter is going to kick my ass for being in his room. And for seeing what I saw.

And they run after me. I run fast. But it isn't fast enough.

***

"Jared, man, what are you doing?" I hear my brother ask.

"Your brother's a snoop. And a faggot. I know what he wants."

My hips are lifted and my shorts and boxers are pulled down exposing my ass. My hard-on flips loose and I feel like I'm going to pee.

"Fuck! Peter, let go, fucker! Fuck!"

And Peter lets go of my wrists and stands up. But I can't run because Jared now has his knees pinning the back of my calves.

"Jared, damn. What are you gonna do?"

"Look at him, Peter. Faggot's got a boner! Did you like what you saw, faggot?"

"I didn't—"

"There was nothin' to see!" my brother squeaks.

I hear a zip and look back. Jared pulls his dick out of his pants and strokes it. It's short, but really thick and a scary purple red.

"Jared, come on. No way. Let's go." My brother says and starts walking towards the cemetery entrance.

"Jared! Come on!" he shouts. "He won't say nothing. Paul won't—"

"Jared, no—" I cry.

And his fist hits the back of my head.

And I hear Peter run away.

And then I feel Jared touch my dick. I think I might shoot. "Jared, don't."

"Don't what, faggot?"

"Don't. I don't want—"

But I did. I was afraid, but I did. His hand feels so good. And I'm going to come. I'm going to come! Then he stops.

"Take off your shorts." He moves his knees and I fall over as pain shoots through my legs. I roll over onto my back with my legs up in the air, my shorts and boxers still around my knees.

Jared pulls my shorts off over my tennis shoes, then my boxers, and grips each of my legs in his hands.

"Ah. Nice faggot. Now I'm gonna give you what you want—"

"Shit, Jared, no. Let me go and I'll suck your—"

"You want to suck my dick, man?" Jared looks down at his dick, then spits out a long hocker, which just hangs there, then finally separates and lands right on his purple dickhead.

"Yeah, Jared. I'll suck your dick. I will! Promise! You don't have—"

He lifts my legs back and my ass opens up. I fart. I feel his dick press against my asshole, then pressure as he tries to slide it in. I feel pain shooting through my gut and legs and I grab onto his shoulders pulling at his t-shirt. Then my dick does shoot. I don't touch it. I don't have to. Having Jared's dick partway into my asshole is enough.

"Aeeeeeeeeeeee—" I scream as my dick explodes and my asshole clamps down even harder around Jared's dickhead than it had been before.

"Ah fuck, Paul! I'm going to shoot!"

Paul? He hadn't ever called me anything but faggot. I feel a tiny pop as his stubby hard-on pulls out then I feel his warm come shooting on the back of my legs.

"Don't ever fucking tell anyone, you shit!" he says, then stands up and tucks his wet and already soft dick into his jeans. "I mean it. Or I'll do it again!"

He takes off. I grab my boxers and wipe up all the come, both his and mine, then put on my shorts. On the way out, I toss my wet boxers into a trashcan.

My brother never mentioned what happened. And I never told him what his friend Jared and I had done. Actually, Peter and I rarely talked again after that afternoon except when forced. Jared never came over to the house again either, and I guess they stopped hanging out because I never saw them together.

I thought of asking my brother about what he and Jared were doing in his room. But I didn't.

I thought of asking Jared if he wanted to do it again. But I didn't. Even though I wanted to.

\*\*\*

"…Breathe slowly and deeply. Visualize the image of Green Tara. Repeat the mantra—"

"The mantra?" I ask.

"Yes, Miss White Tara! Geez, where've you been? The mantra: OM TARE TUTTARE YE SWAHA…"

"Have you seen Jared Bowker at all recently?"

"OHHHHHHHHHM."

"Green Tara! Hello!"

"I heard you! Why do you want to bring up that redneck creep now? I thought you were over him. We're meditating."

"I've just been wondering where he went."

"Don't tell me you still think about doing him again? Come on, White Tara! Paleeze!" She rolls her eyes at me.

"Jen—"

Jennifer reads from the book again, "Imagine a beautiful emerald green light coming out of Tara's heart and flowing like ribbons into your heart…"

I stare up at the tree and my vision blurs and shifts. The tree's branches smooth into arms and a face appears. I see a beautiful emerald green light shining through the blood orange goddess tree.

"…Let yourself be filled with this light as you feel her healing protection all around you."

\*\*\*

*Mary and I float above the apartment I rent in San Francisco. I'm 21 and she would be 19. The fog is rolling in and we are floating in the middle of clouds and I should be cold since I'm naked but I'm not. Mary is wearing a pair of my jeans without a shirt. He breasts are small with bronze-colored cherry-sized nipples. She's wearing a green stone in her belly button. Her hair is waist-length and braided into one long white ponytail. She is eating cotton candy, delicately pulling the spun pink sugar with her fingers and letting it melt on her tongue.*

*"I love him, Mary." I say as we gaze down at my bedroom where I am making love.*

*"I know you do, baby. I know you do. But be careful what you do, big brother."*

*We watch below as my lover Jared slowly moves his hand back and forth inside me. I lay on the bed with my legs over his shoulders and my arms behind me gripping the iron headrest. His hand is inside me and my asshole is tightly clenching around his wrist. His other hand gently rubs my chest and stomach in circles. He is smiling. My eyes are rolled back into my head and I'm making soft moaning sounds like a chant.*

*"Oh, that? It's fine. He's very careful. He knows what he's doing. And I always go into a zone like that when he handballs me."*

*"I know he knows what he is doing, Paul. But do you? Not the sex. Your heart. Be careful of your heart." She pulls off a long length of pink cotton candy and lays it on her tongue. We both look down at the scene in my bedroom. A soft red light hovers over my heart.*

*"Am I going to die? Is that a heart attack like Daddy?"*

*"No, big brother. That's a broken heart. A bad one. A very painful one. I know who that is, Paul. I know how you found him. See…"*

\*\*\*

I'm back in Colma for my mom's funeral. I feel alone. Everyone is dead, or dying in my brother's case, or gone from Colma. I feel like I'm the only one left. Mary hasn't visited for a long time and didn't even show me Mom's death.

The viewing is tonight, but I don't want to go. Not sure why I even came home. Well, I guess it's not really home now. Fine with me. It was bad enough talking to Peter on the phone. I don't really want to see him. He'll be here soon.

I do a line of coke and jump in my wreck of a Honda Civic and drive off before Peter can get there from work. He can handle the viewing alone. Right before the exit for the expressway to San Francisco I spot a carnival.

I pull over quickly and park. I'm at a carnival. How odd. My mom's just died and I'm going to do what? Ride some rides? Not any of these scary rusty ones, that's for sure.

I wish Green Tara was in town. She's my only ally left in Colma. I had called her and left a message as soon as I heard the news about Mom's death, but when she returned my call she said she was in Arizona for a visit with her husband's family and wouldn't be back in time.

I walk though the crowded little midway watching the families and couples play games. It's noisy and cheap and more than a bit scary. I would have loved it when I was in high school with Tara, perhaps high on her mom's brownies. But now it's just crowded and it isn't much fun and I'm high but the coke is just a way to cope.

Then I spot him. Jared. At a booth. He's working in a booth. It's one of those games with fake shotguns and a cardboard wilderness scene where for a dollar you can shoot at some cute little bunnies and ducks and deer, trying to knock down as many as possible to win some prize.

Jared, my brother's fucked-up fuck-buddy in high school. Jared, who raped me in Final Rest Cemetery. Jared, the man who I feared the most, yet dreamed of and desired the most. He's the reason I'm so fucked up — or at least he's who I've always blamed. He's the reason I'm such a slut — or at least he's who I've always blamed. He's the man I always look for in other men, and he's who I see when I close my eyes with the other men.

He looks great. He's filled out some. He appears taller, but his face still looks the same except for a little soul patch gone scraggly. He has on a blue tank top, baggy jeans, and a tight gold chain and crucifix around his neck. His arms are large and covered in tattoos. His hair is shoulder length and greasy, unkept, wild, like I like. Like mine. He is leaning over the low wall of shotguns trying to charm some kids out of their money in exchange for a large stuffed purple Barney. His jeans hang loose but I can almost see his dick's outline where it bulges in front.

I walk over. I should run away but I don't this time. I don't turn around and run to my car. I don't take the exit to the expressway and head back to San Francisco. I walk right up to him and slap down a dollar. He looks up from the gaggle of ten-year-olds to me and smiles.

"Paul? Paul Jackson?"

\*\*\*

*Mary shows me Jared and I later that same evening at his apartment. I'm down on my knees in his living room. We're naked and I have his dick in my mouth and one of my hands on his balls and the other hand pulling on one of his pierced nipples and he's holding my head with both his hands guiding himself in and out and I'm moaning loudly and he's saying my name over and over. It didn't take much convincing to get me to that point and time. I wanted him. I had always wanted him again. Since that first violent time, as sad as that sounds. And he wanted me too.*

*Mary hands me a blood orange she has plucked from somewhere in the clouds. It's overripe and bleeding down her pale arm.*

*"I love him, Mary."*

*"I know. The world is full of love, Paul. It's full of desire. And sex. Yes, sex. Sex that rocks your world. Sex that you want more than anything else and fear more than death. Sex with your body laid down under a headstone taking hate deep within*

*yourself. And sex with a man you've always loved but shouldn't."*

*"But I do love him, Mary. And he —"*

*"I know, honey. I know you do. The world is full of crazy misplaced love and violence and pain and yearning and blood oranges and cotton candy. And you can't change what happened in the past and you can't always see what's coming or control the way things will happen. But be careful, Paul, big brother. Be very careful. This one is gonna break your heart. This one's gonna hurt.*

## HUSBAND, SIRE, IT

*At 39, who would have suspected that I would find sexual bliss? Hasn't it always been a much-repeated fact that a man reaches his sexual prime at 17? How horrible to be just at the beginning of something as wonderful as sexual activity, knowing that it will go downhill from there. At 17, I was certainly very active, but the pleasure then – in fact the pleasures I have enjoyed my entire life – are nothing compared to what I have now. I have found IT.*

*The IT has come after a long-distance courtship via email with SIRE, a writer I've admired for years. Our friendship grew over months of writing, secrets shared, desires admitted to, pictures taken and attached. And then I took a trip to be with SIRE. And I found IT.*

*I live with HUSBAND.*

\*\*\*

The dried rose lies on his bedside table, perched on a pile of books. A single rose, now lacking most of its color and scent, but not the meaning. This rose was a small gift—a surprise—from me while SIRE was on a reading tour. He was in Vancouver, so far away, and I was at home in Chicago wishing I could be with him. I had a friend who lives there deliver it at the reading with a whispered "To SIRE from your boy" message, knowing that hearing those words would be as precious a gift to him as any I could offer.

\*\*\*

*The pressure builds with every day.*

*I jog. I play tennis. I work out. Nothing helps. I think of him every minute as I sweat and sweat and sweat, trying hard to feel release. Nothing helps. I will see him again in a month.*

*I live with HUSBAND.*

\*\*\*

It is my first night with SIRE. I am naked, standing alert and aware—at attention—waiting for the games to begin as he lights candles around his bedroom.

He shows me the way he expects me to always position myself when starting a night of play between SIRE and boy. He then inspects me, whispering firm yet loving descriptions of what he sees and feels. We discuss my "safeword" and what it means, and when—if ever—I should use it. I am shown all the toys he might use to either please or discipline me—including assorted dildoes, clamps, restraints, rope, his new riding crop, soft floggers, not so soft whips, and a cane. The cane, he says, will never be used on my soft beautiful skin, that he doesn't wish to cause that kind of pain, or scar me in that way.

Whispering softly in my ear, he asks what I want. When he speaks this way during play, he sounds very much like an 18th-century lord, much like one of the characters he has created. "What do you want, boy?" Partly from this reverie of him being one of his lordly characters and partly because I am so excited to be here, I smile and stifle a giggle. I tell him only to please him, whatever SIRE desires. The smile is returned.

\*\*\*

*The pressure builds with every day.*

*I hear pop songs from open car windows and take the melodies of love to heart, make them my own. Feel them as if written for me. I am falling in love with SIRE. I will see him again in three weeks.*

*I live with HUSBAND.*

\*\*\*

When I take the position he expects: on all fours, knees spaced far apart, ass spread wide, my mouth and tongue cleaning his boot, I know that I have found IT. I clean his boot with complete attention until I am told that I have done a good job, and start on his second. I then lick every inch of his jeans spending extra time at his crotch, licking until my tongue is dry and scratchy and his crotch completely wet. As instructed, I undress him slowly, enjoying every inch of skin I bare as if I hadn't spent the entire weekend already getting to know it.

I take SIRE's cock in my mouth. I am suddenly very hungry to make him come. I worship his hardness with undying focus, spending time with his balls all the way up to the wonderfully wide piss slit that I lap at heartily, eager to get as much of my tongue inside as I can. I fuck him hard with my mouth, the intent simple, to pleasure him, to feel him buck against me and fill my mouth with his cum. I am almost there; I know this from the way his thickness is building, his balls pulling up tight, his legs slightly shaking. He instructs me to stop and firmly pulls my mouth from his cock, leaving a trail of his precum and my spit down my chin.

\*\*\*

*The pressure builds with every day.*

*I masturbate several times daily to release it. But it doesn't help. I work all night long — editing and writing — and I smoke more and more, hoping to feel the release. But it doesn't help.*

*The pressure is much deeper; a scar is now forming in my heart. A permanent tattoo, more permanent than the marks he leaves when we play, that mark me as his, as belonging to SIRE. I will see him again in two weeks.*

*I live with HUSBAND.*

***

Slowly, methodically, he wraps my body. And I am more than a little afraid—no, nervous. He wraps me in Saran Wrap, like a mummy, until I cannot move. My entire body, except for feet and head, are completely secured. It is a test of my trust. And I do trust him. I trust SIRE. The fear is real, but I am relaxing into it. I love and trust this man more than anyone ever in my life. He tilts me back and lifts me onto his bed, positioning me on my back like a lab specimen that he will now do tests on. And I am so hard. And my skin is so alive.

He then brings out his riding crop, the one he said he kept only for show and that I might never feel, the one that I knew instantly I wanted him to use. He brings it to my lips and I kiss it, the sensation causing me to shiver.

With scissors he slowly cuts out circles around my nipples, and the air hitting them is almost enough to make me cum. My cock pushes and thumps against my second skin. But this wonderful sensation is nothing compared to what I feel when he starts snapping the crop down in quick sharp slaps on first one then the other nipple. IT.

After a few—ten, twenty, sixty?—minutes, he carefully flips me over. The fear rises again, but his voice is soothing, calm, hypnotic. He cuts another patch of the Saran Wrap away. I think I will black out as I feel his breath on my asshole. I writhe trying to bend my ass up without much success and finally just bite down on the bedcover screaming as I feel the first finger touch, then probe. IT.

Eventually, the Saran Wrap skin breaks and pulls apart at spots. My body's writhing and bucking has been too much of a match. At first, I resisted the urges to let go—afraid he would not be pleased if I enjoyed it too much—but these fears were put to rest when he stated he wanted me to receive pleasure, that it is his reward. It is not just for him. It is for me.

The wrapping is slowly cut off and the shock of the cold air paralyzes me. Not what I expected after being so totally restrained, finally free but unable to move. He pulls me to him and I am held tightly and kissed fiercely on my lips, cheeks, and eyelids. I cry and tell Sire that I love him.

***

*The pressure builds with every day.*

*How do I tell my partner of 18 years that I love another? How do I tell HUSBAND that I have found something that he can't offer…and that I need to do this, that…that I love him, but that I need to do this…. How can I tell my best friend this without breaking his heart, his spirit?*

*I will see SIRE next week.*

***

We exchange rings and vows. SIRE and boy. The rings are to be worn when we play. The vows are to be together, forever.

He gives me a present. He lifts each leg and fits my new leather restraints on each ankle. I gladly offer each arm so he can do the same, and I am then tied to each corner of his bed — face down.

The dried rose lies on his bedside table, perched on a pile of books. A single rose, now lacking most of its color and scent, but not the meaning. This rose was a small gift — a surprise — from me while SIRE was on a reading tour. He was in Vancouver, so far away, and I was at home in Chicago wishing I could be with him. I had a friend who lives there deliver it at the reading, with a whispered "To SIRE from your boy" message, knowing that hearing those words would be as precious a gift to him as any I could offer.

It is late and I've lost all track of time. When I realize that he has spent four hours on me, I tell Sire what I experienced — that IT was better than any orgasm. That every time I felt the bite of his whip on my back and shoulders, or of his teeth on my ass and legs, IT intensified. That the sensations I felt while being restrained, having my ass worked over by his mouth and experienced fingers, then by a butt plug and a dildo, and finally by his fat cock, was one very long intense orgasm that was not focused just in my cock and balls, but my entire body and very soul. Pure pleasure. Bliss.

\*\*\*

*I cancel my flight home to HUSBAND. The pressure is gone. In its place is IT.*

# RIDING WITH WALTER

Walter is standing on the seat, his head proudly hanging out the window, his tail wagging with happiness. This is his favorite thing, cruising in my truck with me, teary-eyed in the wind, his muzzle drooling over everything it comes in contact with.

"Where to, huh? What do you say we hit the Dunes today...go for a little road trip? Huh, buddy? Got anything better to do?"

I had to get out of the city. Last night was a blur. One fucking blur. I don't know what got in to me, what I was thinking. Oh, but I do know. That ass. That perfect ass.

It's not like I haven't looked before. Eddie and I spend a lot of time together. He's my sister's husband. So I've looked, checked out the package every so often. He's very handsome, sexy even. I just never thought too much about it. He's married: family. Besides, he always wears big baggy pants.

I pull into traffic heading east to 94 that will take me out of the city and to the Indiana Dunes. My hair feels grainy as I rub my fingers through it. I didn't bathe when I got up, just brushed my teeth, grabbed my cutoffs, my keys, and Walter. Eddie was long gone.

I bring my hand to my face and feel a stirring in my cock as I breathe deep. His smell. All over my hands. His scent so strong on my fingertips: come, sweat, his ass. Like caramel, sweet caramel warming on the stove. I breathe deep, swooning at the smell of his ass on my fingertips...

Shit! I swerve back into my lane before nearly hitting the car next to me! God, that was close. Walter gives me a look like he knows what I was thinking about, then goes back to hanging out the window, drool and all.

"You were no help at all, you know," I snap at Walter as if last night were his fault.

Last night, shit, last night...I can hardly blame Walter though; ignoring me and sleeping next to Eddie like it was natural he was naked in my bed. Like Eddie belonged there.

\*\*\*

*I knew it was him from the stomps on the steps. His footsteps were unmistakable; always hitting the same creaks loudly every time he visited. The same sounds that no one else seemed to make when they climbed the stairs to my second-floor flat. But he did. Every time.*

*I opened the door before he knocked, happy to see him.*

*"What's up, Eddie?" My smile quickly dropped once I saw his sad face and puffy red eyes.*

*"She left, John. She left me. Well, not for good, I don't think. Just tonight, she went to your folks'. She's pissed, real pissed. I think I pushed her too far this time."*

*He cried on my shoulder and I, uncomfortably, did my best to comfort him through four Coronas each, a pack of Camels, and three hours of reruns on Nick-at-Nite. He genuinely didn't understand why my sister was pissed off. He wanted kids, now, and she didn't. Christ, she was just made a partner at her firm. She didn't have time. And I don't think she was ready. But Eddie was old-fashioned Latino, from a large family, and ready for her to pop out some kids.*

*I finally tired and told him to stay with me instead of driving home. I made up the couch, tucked him in like a five-year-old, and went to bed more than a little tipsy.*

*I'm not sure what time it was when I had to pee. Tip-*

toeing through the living room, I made it to the bathroom without a sound. On my way back through, I looked over at my guest. The streetlights were shining through the venetian blinds, lighting the room and Eddie asleep on his stomach, the sheet kicked aside and his perfect brown butt cheeks in full view.

My god, they were perfect! Chiseled mounds of dimpled porno-star-quality bubble-butt just staring at me. I froze. He looked so angelic. I could almost imagine the billowy white angel wings sprouting from his shoulder blades. A beautiful brown angel asleep on my couch.

Without thinking, my hand went to my cock and stroked it through my briefs. He looked so good. So good! I reached inside and wrapped my hand around my growing hard-on, wondering what his cock looked like when I saw them move. Not just move; they were flexing. His ass cheeks were flexing. My mind was slow to realize what my eyes were seeing. Then I looked at his face and saw him watching me. Watching me jerking off watching him!

Oh shit! But he was smiling. A smile unlike any I'd ever seen from Eddie. This one was wicked. Absolutely wicked.

He didn't say anything, just slowly stretched his body out full, then readjusted himself lifting his ass into the air and reaching under to obviously stroke his cock. His ass cheeks bobbed in the air, calling my name, taunting me.

I didn't think, I just moved. Not to the bedroom as you would assume, but to the couch and straight to his ass. His big beautiful ass that he was obviously offering me. I wasn't thinking of Eddie and my sister. My sister didn't exist. Just Eddie. And Eddie's large, muscled ass dancing just inches from my face. And what I intended to do to it.

Before my face even found its target, I heard him moan. Long and deep, as if he were in ecstasy. My cock jerked in its confinement. Then my lips grazed his ass, first up one smooth cheek then the other, until my nose, full of his heavy scent, guided my mouth to the puckered hole. A first date kiss. Gentle and soft, then more needy, finally exploring his asshole with my tongue. Hungry and deep, as if I hadn't eaten in days and he was my meal.

\*\*\*

With one hand on the wheel, I unbutton my cutoffs and free my stiff cock. I begin pumping hard, trying my best to keep my eyes focused on the road, my pre-come dripping in anticipation over my fist. I lick my lips, the taste of him still there or possibly just imagined at this point. Oh, Eddie! I pull harder and harder, stretching my cock's skin for all it's worth, my foot pressing against the gas pedal, trying to outrun my desire and last night. To outrun my thoughts of Eddie.

\*\*\*

*I came the first time without even touching myself, both my hands under his body, between his legs, jerking on his brown thick cock as one, my tongue fucking his asshole. When he came, he cried out my name loudly, repeatedly, his ass constricting over and over around my tongue, his cock furiously pumping into my fists. And he came. And I came. And came.*

\*\*\*

What am I gonna do? I think as my orgasm builds up in my balls. What can I do? Nothing. We'll both pretend it didn't happen. He didn't let me eat his ass out. He didn't let me jerk him off. I didn't lick the come from his body, didn't kiss his sweet mouth.

"What am I gonna do, Walter?"

We'll pretend that he didn't get hard and come again, this time inside my mouth. And he didn't stick his large fingers up my ass and fuck me with them while I shot all over his chest and neck. We didn't fall asleep spooned together on my bed like we were in love. We'll pretend it didn't happen. Maybe we'll just pretend it didn't happen!

When I shoot, my come splatters all over the wheel and the dashboard. The speedometer reads 85 as I cross the Indiana state line. We're almost to the dunes, the beach, and a swim. I relax my foot to a steady 65, and rub my come into my cutoffs and skin as best as I can.

I'm still hard so I leave my cock out. I'm still hard and thinking of Eddie. I'm thinking about Eddie and my sister. I'm thinking of Eddie and his sweet ass. His sweet delicious ass. I suck my fingers pretending they're his. And I'm thinking about what I'm gonna do about the mess I've gotten myself into when I pull into the lot at the beach and park.

I'm already wondering when I can taste him again. I need to taste him again. I bring my sticky fingers to my lips.

Walter hasn't moved from his favorite spot. He's still standing on the seat, his head proudly hanging out the window, his tail wagging with happiness, teary-eyed from the wind, his muzzle drooling all over the side of my truck.

# CAMPING

It's Saturday night, 1:30 in the morning, mid-July, 1976. I'm wide-awake in a tent at the Indiana Dunes with my best friend Daniel, his little sister June, and his parents.

Daniel and I have been giggling for about two hours every time his Mom lets out a snore or his Dad lets out a big rip of a fart.

I'm fifteen, and Daniel is sixteen. I have a hard-on and I have to pee.

His Dad lets out a squealer and we start cracking up.

"Sssshhh…"

"Hey, Daniel, I gotta take a leak, come with me," I whisper.

"No way, faggot, it's too far to the flush toilets, and the others stink too much! Go by yourself."

I punch him for calling me a faggot and stumble out of the tent, stepping on June who lets out only a little squeak.

I head out with the flashlight focused on the road ahead of me. It's really dark, and the fog makes it hard to see anything but just the few feet in front of me. Although I laughed earlier at Daniel's dad's story of the infamous camping ax-murderer, I find myself regretting my decision to take the longer walk to the shower building for a less stinky pee. The darkness is complete, and I begin to feel that there really is someone or something just out of sight, waiting for me.

I fish from my pocket one of the two remaining smashed cigarettes I brought for Daniel and me to sneak over the weekend and light it. Fuck him, he didn't want to come! The walk takes about ten minutes because I take a wrong turn and have to go around a second time. I really have to pee!

When I finally make out the lights of the shower building, I have nearly forgotten the ax-murderer and the fact that he had been lurking right outside my flashlight's beam. All I can think about is getting to a urinal.

I jump into the bright lights and head right to the urinals. I hear a spray of water and think that this is definitely the time to shower with nobody around to see you naked. I step up and pull out my dick. It comes out hard in my hand, and I realize I'll never squeeze a pee out this way.

The decision to jerk myself off in one of the shower stalls is quick and easy, and I pull my shirt down over my boner and rush to the stalls. It will only take me a couple minutes to jerk off, and then I can pee. I pass the first stall and am startled to see that the plastic drape is only half closed, allowing me to get a complete view of a naked guy soaping himself up. Yikes! I rush past the stall, hoping he didn't see me looking, and jump in the last one with all my clothes on.

I pull my cutoffs and underwear down to my ankles and start to pump my boner. I start thinking of the story Daniel told me last week, about the blow job he said a girl gave him here last summer. I imagine him standing with his own cutoffs around his ankles as her head bounces up and down on his hard dick.

I'm startled from my vision as I notice too late that there is movement outside the shower drape. The guy from the other shower stall is right outside mine, and I can see him drying off through the space the drape doesn't cover. Crap! Did he see me? Why'd he move down so far?

I watch as he spreads his legs and wipes at his ass with his towel. He's only a couple years older than I am, but he's really hairy and his dick looks so big. It's larger than my hard-on by inches and it's not even really hard. I'm tall for my age, and without much to compare it to, I thought my dick was big! I hold it still with my hand, afraid I'll shoot. I take a deep breath and hold it, but forget to exhale and get dizzy. My sneakers slip out from underneath me and I bang against the side of the hollow metal of the stall with a loud thud.

"Shit!" I scream and he pulls the drape aside and looks in.

"You okay, guy?"

"Yeah, great." What can I say? I'm standing there with my pants down and my dick in my hand! Busted.

He looks at me a minute, and then smiles wide. Here it comes! He's gonna rat on me, or maybe something worse! I notice that he has dropped his towel, and his dick has started to grow larger, bobbing a little on its own.

I hold my breath as he steps into the stall and says, "Do you want some help with that? I don't want you to hurt yourself."

I'm speechless, so he takes that as a "yes," which I guess it was, and leans in, grabbing my head and pulling my mouth to his. I think I'm going to black out from the feeling of his lips on mine. That and the fact that I forgot to start breathing again. But the feeling doesn't last long because he lifts me up so I'm standing, then kneels down in front of me. Oh my god! I gulp in air.

He takes my stiff dick in his mouth and swallows me whole. My legs shake as he grabs my ass cheeks and pumps me into his mouth. I don't know what to do with my hands, so I lay them on his shoulders. It doesn't take long before I shoot jizz for the first time into the mouth of a man, well, anyone. I'm dizzy again, and my legs are still shaking, as he takes his tongue and licks the length of my dick. I almost fall down, again, tripping on the entangled shorts around my feet, and bang against the metal with another echoing thud. Damn!

He stands up. I watch in wonder as he pulls on

the amazing length of his own boner, it has to be six inches long! He yanks on it hard and fast, and lets out a "Oh, fuck!" as he shoots all over my stomach and legs. Wow! I realize too late what I've missed out on, but I step out of the shorts at my feet so I can kneel down in front of him anyway.

"Oh, yeah," he says as I tentatively put the enormous head into my mouth and taste his jizz. Not what I thought it would taste like, but still good. My heart is beating so hard I think it will burst. I do my best to swallow more of his boner when the loud bang of the front door stops me, mid-dick. It's a good thing I have his dick in my mouth, because I would have screamed out. I suddenly have to pee again, and grab my still-hard boner to stop it from happening here in the shower.

All I can think is "Shit, what are we going to do? What if it's a ranger!" and he lifts me up and pulls me to him quickly as he tugs the drape closed.

He winks at me and whispers, "Ssshhh..."

We listen as this man intrudes on our privacy, whistling as he strips down and noisily gets into the stall next to ours. He turns on the water and continues to whistle as he bathes. I hear his soap drop and bounce around the stall. I start giggling and put my hand over my mouth.

I'm a little scared, but my new friend pulls me closer to him, and puts his lips to mine again. He tastes so good, like he just brushed his teeth, and I soon find myself feeling more self-assured in my kissing. I have my arms around his neck as we lick at each other's tongues, and his arms are down around my back, pulling on my ass. I want him to do more than kiss me, which he does. His big middle finger pushes up inside me, and I let out a muffled "Oh!" into his mouth. Ouch! I'm not sure that's what I had in mind, and it surprises me.

He readjusts his body against mine as he slowly moves his finger in and out of my ass. I feel his dick, still hard, rubbing up on my stomach and decide that next time I won't miss out. I want him to shoot jizz in my mouth.

The man from the next stall is still whistling as he dries himself off and then we hear the bang of the front door as he exits.

My friend gives one final thrust of his finger with a smile and then pulls it out of me. I immediately go down onto my knees. I wrap my hand around the base of his throbbing dick and study it for a moment deciding what to do before placing my mouth back on its head. It seems so big — compared to mine and my friends' dicks anyway — I can barely get half of it in my mouth before gagging. So I try harder, determined to make him feel as good as he made me.

"Don't try so hard, guy", he says as he pulls my head off it. "Just suck on my big head, or lick it. Yeah, like that…lick it."

So I do. I lick it. He grabs himself and slowly pumps the skin on his shaft back and forth as I slurp greedily on it. The head of his dick seems to double in size in my mouth as I take my own hard-on back in hand and jack it.

"You do that great. I'm gonna shoot again soon. Now suck it. Are you ready for me to shoot? Are you ready?"

I answer by shooting my own wad up into the air. I see stars, literally, as he grabs the back of my head and pumps his dick in and out of my eager mouth. He bangs at the back of my throat and squirts. I gag and try to pull off. I can't believe how much jizz is filling my mouth. I panic. I have to pull off but he holds my head. Unsure of what to do, I just swallow. Oh my god! I just swallowed his jizz! I gag again and wipe at my face as tears fall down my cheeks, but I don't stop.

After what seems like a gallon of jizz, he pulls out and steps back. He says, "Man that was great. I should go, my folks will be wondering where I am. What's your name, guy?"

I wipe at my mouth with my arm. "Tom. I, ah —"

"I'm Gary. Thanks!"

That's it?

We both dress, and take off in separate directions. I light the remaining cigarette and the flashlight, and slowly walk back to the tent, not once thinking about the infamous camping ax-murderer or the fact that earlier I had worried about being his next victim. I realize I never peed, so I just turn off the flashlight and pee on a bush by the side of the road.

I think about what just happened. I think about what I've been feeling for a long time now. I've wanted to have sex with another guy, and now I have! I liked it. I think about how good it felt to let Gary put his dick in my mouth. I think about my friend Daniel, and wonder what he would taste like if we did it. I put Daniel's head on Gary's body, and I suck him. I pretend his dick is as big as Gary's and suck him. I let him shoot in my mouth. I think of tomorrow night, and that I will make Daniel go with me to the showers so I can do him!

I'm thinking about Daniel's dick in my mouth all the way back to the tent and as I fall asleep next to him, his sister, and his snoring and farting parents, with the taste of Gary's jizz still strong in my mouth.

I never did find out how Daniel's dick tasted. We unexpectedly left the next morning, and I was always too chicken to do more than just wrestle with him. After that night, I was even too embarrassed to get dressed in front of him, afraid he would see my hard-on, which was always at attention when I was with him.

After a while, we didn't even wrestle. We both made new friends. He got a girlfriend who he spent all his time with. Gary was my first and only experience until I was seventeen, when I found another friend from school who wanted what I did.

I took him camping.

# BUTTERFLIES AND MYTHS

*Legend has it that whispering a wish to a butterfly and then releasing it to carry the wish to the heavens will make the wish come true.*

***

I kiss Trebor good night. A soft kiss on his scruffy cheek, then a whispered *I love you* into his ear. We are snuggled up close in our bed, him on his back, jaw slightly open, softly snoring, and me on my side, watching the profile of the man I love sleep. Trebor's face is so sweet, almost prepubescent, with smooth soft skin, a striking contrast to how hairy my Bear man is. His pretty baby face defies his age — just last week celebrating his 45$^{th}$ birthday — and the only hint to who he used to be.

It hasn't fully hit me yet, the emotions slow to catch up with the news that we will be separated for three months. He broke the news to me earlier tonight while we ate dinner.

"I got the *Geographic* grant," Trebor says while noisily chewing a mouthful of spinach salad.

"The Geod—" I hadn't heard him clearly.

"Yeah…NO! The *Geographic* grant! For my Itzpapálotl expedition to Mexico for the winter!"

"No shit? That's great, babe," I say, hoping I sound cheerful even though I realize this means travel for him, and separation anxiety for me. I'm selfish. I can't help it. I didn't think he would actually go and I don't want his research to take him away from me.

"Don't be that way." His face is blushing red. It always turns blotches of red when he has to deal with my childish emotions. We've been together just over a year and he is just now beginning to truly know my emotional mood swings. I'm what he calls a live wire, my emotions quick to jump from one extreme to another.

My face must have said it all. "What way am I—"

"You know what this means to me. It'll only be three months. Three months. What's that mean in the big picture? We talked about this already, baby. You knew I was planning to go and that I was hoping the grant could make it happen."

"I know," I say while pushing my plate away. Chewing on my lips and trying not to make eye contact, I pour us both more Protocolo, our favorite Spanish red wine. God, why did I have to act like such a child instead of the 30-year-old adult I was supposed to be.

Trebor has degrees in zoology, entomology, and tropical agriculture from Oxford, London and Reading Universities. He has studied *Lepidoptera*—butterflies and moths—most of his life and has collected throughout Europe, Africa, the Indian Ocean Islands, and most of North, Central, and South America. He's become one of the world's top experts on butterflies, specifically those in North America.

The *Geographic* grant covers the cost of an expedition to travel throughout Mexico, not to collect butterflies, but to collect and catalog the history of butterflies, including ancient Mexico's beliefs about the winged beasts and several goddesses, including the Aztec goddess Itzpapálotl. This would take about four months total—three of those in Mexico—for all the traveling and cataloging, before being finally being published. It was very important to Trebor and I was being a brat, but I couldn't stop myself.

"Look—"

"No! You look!" I scream, throwing my plate at the sink. It lands with a thud, instead of the crash I had wanted. "Shit! I'm sorry, Treb, I—"

"I know, Travis. I know. I'm going to miss you something crazy. We'll get you tickets to come for a week in January. How 'bout over New Year's? Ring in the new year in MEHEEKO? You can get away from the deep freeze for a little while. It'll do you good. I'm not going away for good, okay? I'm not leaving you. It's my job."

And that was it. Trebor's leaving for the winter.

\*\*\*

*Many ancient civilizations believed that butterflies were symbols of the human soul.*

*The Greeks believed that a new human soul was born each time an adult butterfly emerged from its cocoon; Northern Europeans believed that dreams were the result of the soul-butterfly's wanderings through other worlds; and in Southern Germany, some believed that the dead were reborn as children who flew about as butterflies. The Irish believed that butterflies were the souls of the dead waiting to pass through purgatory, and the Shoshone that butterflies were originally pebbles, into which the Great Spirit blew the precious breath of life. The Blackfeet believed that dreams were brought to us in sleep by butterflies; the Maya that butterflies were the spirits of dead warriors in disguise descended to earth; the Aztecs that the happy dead in the form of beautiful butterflies would visit their relatives to assure that all was well.*

*And the Nagas of Assam believed the dead went through a series of transformations in the underworld finally to be reborn as a butterfly. When the butterfly died, that was the end of the soul forever.*

\*\*\*

"How was your day, lovely man?" He asks me as soon as I walk through the door.

I had been very sad and grumpy all day. And my job as *Grantwriting Assistant III* at the University of Minnesota-Twin Cities is stressful enough, even when I'm not in a sour mood. My day had sucked.

"It sucked," I said giving him my best pouty-boy look.

"Sorry. You hungry? Or can I help you relax a little before dinner?"

His bright eyes, naughty devil smile, and deep sexy voice — as well as the thick cock he is packing down his left pants leg — instantly make me feel better. Food is the furthest thing from my mind. I need a good hard fuck.

Trebor leads me into the bedroom. He strips me of my clothes. The touch of his fingers as they graze my bare skin sends shivers up and down my body. I lie back on our bed with my arms over my head and my legs spread wide, hoping that he is as hungry for my asshole as it is for him.

He's taunting me, making me ache as each layer of clothing is slowly and methodically stripped away: boots, socks, sweatshirt, t-shirt, belt, then finally jeans. He leaves his briefs on, his cock looking painfully tight and stretching the cotton like a tent, the bright white of the briefs a nice contrast to his olive skin and dark fur.

"Show me your hole." His voice rumbles and a shiver literally shakes my body.

I do as he says, lifting my knees up and back so that my asshole is exposed and open.

"Ah, that's nice. So nice," he purrs as he rubs his finger lightly over my shaved pucker.

"Nnnnhhhhuuuhhhh —" I groan.

"You like?"

"Mmmmmmm…yes…fuck…"

And his finger forces in. No lube. No warning.

"YAAAAAAAAAANNNHHEEEEEEEEEEEEEEEYYY!"

"Good boy," he says as he slides it back out. "Good boy."

Trebor rubs his hand up and down over his hard

cock suggestively, making sure I know what he intends to do with it. And I'm ready. So ready.

"Baby—"

"Shhhhhh...not yet, pretty man. Not yet." He opens up the bedside table's top drawer and pulls out our bag of collected plastic, wood, and metal tit clamps. My asshole constricts a few times at the sight and I draw in my breath.

"Ahh...you like?" He dips his hand in and pulls out a silver and black toothed clamp, opens it, and then lightly rubs the teeth over my nipple causing it to instantly harden.

I reach back with both arms and grip at the headboard's railings just as he likes me too. He thinks of it as a nice cruel touch to make me hold myself in position without any actual constraints—though we do use them from time to time—and to make me conquer the urge to move out of position on my own.

"Very nice. Very nice indeed," he states. The metal clip is dropped back into the bag and he pulls out two tiny pink plastic clips. Clips I know well. Clips that are misleading in their looks as to how much pain—and pleasure—they can inflict. He puts the bag on top of the table.

Trebor quickly snaps them down onto the very tip of each nipple and my entire body stiffens. Pain shoots through one end of my body to the other like a bright white light. I try to breathe deep and focus. I close my eyes. Breathe deep and focus. Breathe deep and focus. To let the intense sensation warm through me and to let the endorphins take over.

"Now, let me see that hole again."

I must have been too slow. He takes each clip in his hands and twists.

I'm on fire. I thrash my body and holler bloody murder, but continue to hold onto the bedframe. My cock is so hard. I open my eyes and look down and watch it bounce up and down as if possessed. I pull my knees slowly up toward my chest. Baby, please…

"Baby, please…"

God, put your finger in me now!

"…put your finger in me."

Trebor reaches back into the drawer, his eyes never leaving mine, the sneer I know as desire growing on his lips, and pulls out the lube.

"Such a beautiful hole. I will put my finger in you. And I want you to be a good boy and come for me. I think you can do that, huh?" He squeezes a generous glob of ForPlay into his palm and rubs it between his fingers. "Look at that cock. Look at it! What a porn-star cock you have. It's huge! I bet I can make you come without touching it. Wouldn't that be nice?"

It does look huge. I'm so hard, so ready, so wanting him in me. He *will* be able to make me come without touching my cock. He has before.

"Who's ass is this?" He asks, then climbs up on the bed kneeling in front of my ass and legs, immediately smearing my asshole with the handful of lube. "Is this mine?"

"Ya…yes—" I try to answer as his middle finger slides in, slowly, one knuckle at a time, until it is buried deep inside. "AAAAAAAAAH," is all I can manage.

Trebor knows me well. He knows every inch of my body, inside and out. He knows what to do to give us both the most pleasure. For me, that is having his talented fingers up my ass, massaging my prostate, and to look up into his eyes and realize that that is what gives him the most pleasure.

"Mmmm…how's that…good?" And he wiggles his finger back and forth slightly, making my cock both leap and leak furiously. I lift my knees back further to open up as wide as I can and bump one of the clips. I shake as a body orgasm erupts though me.

Since I've met Trebor, I've developed the most wonderful thing: I can have body orgasms—what many men, I suppose, spend years trying to develop with tantric sex. With me, it just happens. Well, Trebor's fingers *make* it happen.

I look down between my legs at Trebor. His cock is standing straight up in his briefs, and I know that tonight he will fuck me. I need it. I need more. More contact. Rougher. Harder. Enough to hold me during his trip away from me.

His eyes are piercing a hole through me as he methodically rubs my insides, first one, and finally two fingers, pressing and exploring my prostate. I can't take my eyes from his and he starts plunging his fore and middle finger in and out in steady full strokes, each time hitting right on target and rolling over my spot. I am now moaning, long and unintelligibly, trying to lift my ass higher onto his hand, to feel more of him. More of him. More.

"Mmmmmmnnnnmmm…"

"That's it, baby. That's it. Come for me, Travis—"

"Mmmmmmnnnnmmm…"

"Come for me!" And he jabs hard, both fingers fully inside, and at the same time his other hand lifts and twists my right clipped nipple.

My mind explodes in harsh light, my eyes squeeze shut, and my ass clamps down hard around his fingers. My cock shoots, warm bullets of my come flying through the air and hitting my belly, chest, and his arm and hand.

"AAAAAHHHHHHHH!"

And again.

"AAAAAHHHHHHHH!"

And he pulls his fingers out of my asshole's tight ring then forces them roughly back in.

"AAAAAHHHHHHHH!"

And I look down at him as my final burst of come propels from my cock, hitting me on my chin. I start laughing, partly from the amazing sensation of release, and partly from my ability at 30 to still come like a teenager.

Trebor joins me with a robust giggle and roll of his eyes, then lets his fingers slowly slide out.

The orgasm is amazing, still flowing through me

like electricity, still causing my cock and asshole to twitch in unison. But I know the evening is just beginning.

"Be right back," Trebor says, climbing off the bed, his heavy cock flopping in his briefs, heading to the bathroom.

His back is a blaze of color. He spent several thousand dollars, and a great deal of time and pain, having his back tattooed as a reward for landing his first research grant to collect and classify butterfly and moth species in Belize. It's magnificent: a full-color clearly detailed rendering of a monarch butterfly, spreading from shoulder to shoulder, side to side, from neck to waist.

The colors are vivid, still bright after many years, only slightly toned down from the hair he so proudly grows, downy soft, but thickly, over his shoulders and back. As he walks the movement of his shoulders and jiggle of his love handles and cute little ass make it appear to fly.

I watch him walk — and his monarch fly — down the hall to the bathroom.

"Gotta pee. Don't go anywhere."

No worry about that. Nothing could tear me from this spot.

\*\*\*

*Butterflies belong to a group of insects with a complete metamorphosis. This means that there is a pupal stage and that the immature butterfly is morphologically different from an adult butterfly.*

*Metamorphosis can be described as a life cycle. It is a cycle, so it can be very hard to say where it begins, and ends.*

\*\*\*

My ass is buzzing and a little sore.

Trebor returns from the bathroom to find me still in the same position.

"How do you feel?" he asks.

"Mmmm…I'm humming."

"And that sweet ass of yours?" He grabs each of my ankles in his palms and pulls me closer to the edge of the bed, pulling the sheets with me and making me giggle like a child being tickled. "Ready for more?"

I am.

Trebor pulls off his briefs and his thick cock springs free, bouncing up and smacking against his belly as it catches the elastic waistband, then settling down to its natural hard horizontal state. He strokes it firmly, a look of extreme lust coming from his eyes.

I reach over to the table and grab the bottle of lube, hand it to him, then scoot myself closer to the edge of the bed, my ass hanging over the side, my legs straight into the air.

"Fuck me, baby."

The bottle makes a rude farting noise as he squeezes out a generous portion of lube onto his cock's head. We both laugh, and he strokes his now slippery cock and aims it at my wide-open hole.

"How rude!" he announces. Firmly grasping each foot's ankle in his warm strong palms, he lifts my legs fully up and apart, then expertly slides, inch by inch, into me.

"Rude!" I loudly agree, more on auto-drive at this point than anything else. It feels so good, so fucking good.

Trebor growls with each full grinding thrust. My asshole is completely dilated from his talented fingering earlier, so there is little resistance, just pure pleasure.

I grip his shoulders with both hands as he continues to plunge into me. I pull my neck and head up so I can watch his face as he fucks me.

I'm so lucky. God, I'm lucky. Trebor is so beautiful. Look at him!

"OH, FUCK YEAH, BABY! FUCK ME! FUCK ME!"

I wrap one hand firmly over the back of his strong neck for support, and let my other hand glide over his densely woven chest of hair, at first softly touching each of his large pink nipples, the areolas so large, pink and feminine against his masculine dark fur, such beautiful contrast, then more firmly, pinching and pulling first one nipple, then the other, until they proudly poke out.

"FUCK ME! FUCK ME!"

And he accepts my offer, slamming harder, each time almost pulling his cock completely out, then quickly burying it fully with a slight lift, knowing it will hit my sweet spot each time.

"I LOVE—"

And harder, so that each thrust actually lifts me off the bed. I have to let go of his nipple.

"I LOVE—"

And harder. And faster. Trebor's face is now totally focused. He's drilling me with short, very fast, and rough, jabs.

"I LOVE YOU!" I scream.

Without missing a beat, he pulls my feet together so he can grip them as one, and uses his free hand to yank on my cock. Forgetting that it had already come once tonight, it's hard and begging to do it again.

"I love you too, lover," Trebor sings to me.

I let myself relax back onto the bed, Trebor in complete control of my body and its actions. My left hand flails in the air, probably comical to see, almost as if I'm a rodeo rider on a wild bull, using my arm for balance, each brutal thrust into my body met with an equal reaction of the arm over and over.

My right hand reaches underneath to Trebor's cock, to my stretched-out asshole, and where they are both now joined in earnest friction.

My orgasm is building, and all I can do is let out short and loud "AH AH AH!" noises as I feel his every inch pound into me.

I'm going to come. Oh, God!

"AH AH AH!" I shout.

And they are starting to be matched by Trebor.

"ANH ANH ANH!" He's ready to come as well.

I worm my fingers in under the cock's harness, careful of not getting pinched. I know him well: Trebor is very sensitive. It's better not to handle him too roughly. Instead, I just wiggle my fingers, then my complete hand up and underneath his cock so that he is pounding directly against my hand.

"ANH ANH ANH!"

"AH AH AH!"

"AAAAAARRRRRRRRRNNNNN!" and my sweet Bear's engorged clit bangs and bangs, hard, fast, and fierce, against my hand, coming, he is coming, his cunt wet and warm, hard clit extended and oversensitive, banging against my hand, his body trying its best to continue both the plowing of my ass and the stroking of my cock, but he's shaking, every inch of him shaking and nearly convulsing.

"AH AH AH AAAAAARRR!" and I'm coming. The volume of my come is less since I have just come an hour earlier, but the sensation is stronger as my asshole grips, its ring clamping down tight and then releasing and clamping down and releasing upon Trebor's thick cock. He strokes my cock until satisfied I am done.

My ass squeezes him out, and Trebor falls on top of me. We shift our bodies back onto the bed and curl up around each other, my back spooned in against him. We stay like that for a long time, Trebor still wearing his harness and cock, positioned up under my ass and balls, just holding each other, both sticky and wet, him kissing the back of my neck and shoulders, and me just letting the electricity flow out of me through my hands and feet, enjoying the sensations, and enjoying having Trebor hold me close.

\*\*\*

*Unlike most other insects in temperate climates, monarch butterflies cannot survive a long cold winter. Instead, they spend the winter in roosting spots. Monarchs west of the*

*Rocky Mountains travel to small groves of trees along the California coast. Those east of the Rocky Mountains fly farther south to the forests high in the mountains of Mexico. The monarch's migration is driven by seasonal changes.*

*No other butterflies migrate like the monarch. They travel much farther than all other tropical butterflies, up to three thousand miles. They are the only butterflies to make such a long, two-way migration every year.*

\*\*\*

Trying not to cry, I lay my hand and head on his chest. I want him to go, of course, it is the chance of a lifetime, but I will miss him terribly. One more evening of being able to rub my hand through his thick chest hair, and smell his comforting musky body scent while I fall asleep, then he will be gone. I whisper my wish *please come home soon* into his ear, then fall asleep, my head on his chest rising and falling with his breath, my hand cupped over his furry belly, confused and slightly afraid of how I will handle the separation, short as it may be, yet knowing in my heart that he will, indeed, return.

# BLUE

I moved to Chicago several months ago for a job with a design firm and rented this great apartment close to Foster Beach. I bought a cat that I named Cat. Everything was going well, but I was lonely. And horny. I was having what you might call a slump, a dry spell. That was until this last week when I started seeing Blue.

I'm a creature of habit. I roll, well, actually crawl, out of bed at 6:45 every morning after slamming the snooze on my alarm several times. I grab my glasses off the bedside table and stumble to the kitchen barefoot in my boxers where I attack the difficult task of feeding Cat. I'm not what you would call a morning person.

I light my first cigarette and fight with the espresso machine until it cooperates and produces my first caffeine fix of the day. I then light another cigarette and head into the bathroom to put in my contacts. I proceed with the exciting tasks of relieving myself, and shaving. About halfway through the shower, I usually wake up.

The first morning I saw Blue I was only halfway through my first cigarette when I happened to look out my kitchen window and noticed him walking through his kitchen. My window faces the back of another apartment, presumably the same as mine. I hadn't ever seen anyone in it before since the blinds had always been closed and the man out of nowhere startled me.

I watched him as he stopped at his counter and poured himself some coffee. He was wearing only bright blue briefs, and he had a roaring hard-on. Forgetting my half-smoked fag in the ashtray, and my now-cooling espresso, I focused my eyes, surprisingly awake, on the show. Guess he didn't notice me because I hadn't turned on my lights yet. Cool.

The man turned around and leaned back against the counter. His hair was black, or maybe dark brown, and was cut in a short military style. He rubbed his cock through his briefs. He was tall and had a nice trim body. Just the way I like them: long and slim. His large hands rubbed back and forth across his bulge. Even with the twenty-some feet and two windows between us, I could make out every detail of his cock.

I rubbed my own very hard cock, and decided I had to go with this great luck while I had it and shed my boxers. Never one to be brave and actually do it in public or at a club, I figured "what the fuck" since I was in my own kitchen. Though not as long as his, my cock is thick. I immediately started stroking it with both hands as I leaned back against my counter and watched him do the same.

As he pulled his briefs slowly down, his nicely veined cock sprung to freedom with a snap and slapped up against his belly. He took it in his right hand and stroked it while his left hand explored his chest, finding a nipple and pinching himself. I closed my eyes for a moment and tried to remember what a cock tasted like.

He stopped stroking just long enough to taste his coffee, and his long cock stood at attention, curving up into the air. He then went back to his hard-on with caffeinated zeal. He cupped his hairy balls with his left hand and jerked his length with his right. He spread his legs wider and lifted his head until it seemed he was looking straight into my eyes, then shot his load. It flew out into the air, landing what looked to be about five feet away. He pumped again, and shot another load just as far.

This was unbelievable. I was watching my own private sex show! In my kitchen at 7:00 in the morning! I fucked my fist as hard as I could and screamed out as I now shot halfway across the kitchen, almost catching Cat still doing her "I'm hungry, damn it" dance.

I closed my eyes while I jerked on my cock a few more times. When I opened them, he was gone. I fed Cat, poured my now cold espresso into a cup, wiped my mess up with a paper towel, and lit another cigarette.

What just happened?

I went into the bathroom, feeling happier than I had since I had moved here, and got ready for work.

What a way to start the day!

\*\*\*

That night when I returned home after a bitch of a long day, my mystery neighbor's blinds were once again closed. I spent the entire evening peeking my head around the corner to see if he had lifted them. I finally went to bed and jerked off, imagining what I would do with a cock like his, and wondering if I'd only dreamt this morning's adventure.

\*\*\*

I awoke the next morning and stumbled into the kitchen as I had every other morning for the last several months, only this time I had someone waiting for me.

Yikes, I forgot!

Blue was already there with hard-on in hand, staring right at me. His blue briefs were pulled down around his hips. This time I knew he could see me. He was looking right at me with a nasty smile on his lips and his cock was at full attention. I froze. He must have known I was watching yesterday!

I flipped on the lights and tentatively slipped my boxers off. We locked eyes and slowly started a mutual jerk-off. We came at the same time, ejaculating straight toward the other's kitchen.

\*\*\*

My mornings the rest of the week changed. I would wake up earlier and get to the bathroom first to make sure I didn't have bed hair or anything crusty and dried on my face. I would put in my contacts and then run fully awake into the kitchen. Despite her whining, I would ignore feeding Cat her breakfast until I was done with Blue.

He arrived each morning in his same blue briefs, but our activity got more intricate.

Yesterday, he came in as usual and we had our foreplay of rubbing cocks through underwear. He pulled his briefs off and took his long cock in hand. I followed suit. He turned his face to his left and raised his arm. He made an exaggerated smelling motion. This was hot, very hot, and I imagined my face buried in his armpit. I closed my eyes and tried to smell it.

Blue then hopped up on the counter that faced the window. He spread his legs, and I got a beautiful view of his hairy balls hanging low and the full length of his cock standing straight up in the air above them. As all our encounters before had been in unison, I quickly lifted myself onto the counter and assumed the same position.

He spread his legs wider, resting one leg on the other counter by his sink. He slumped down a little with his back against the cupboards so his ass hung over the edge and reached under with his left hand. With two fingers, he spread his cheeks right at the pucker. I was so excited my cock almost erupted right then. I wished I were there to put my mouth on it, to taste his ass. I wanted to lick it, to stick my tongue in his hole and chow down.

I followed suit, but lifted both legs into the air and used my hands to spread my ass as far as it would go. He started pumping his long cock with strong fast strokes as he watched. I continued to hold my ass open for his viewing pleasure, with my legs straight up into the air, not even thinking about the fact I could easily fall off the counter. My cock was leaking and my balls ached. I needed to shoot soon. I let go with my left hand and rubbed my fingers up my dick, collecting my spilled juice and wiped it on my tongue. With a huge grin, I leaned my head back and imagined it was him.

He stuck his middle finger in his mouth and sucked on it. He then placed it back under his ass and inserted it completely up his hole with one motion. His head jerked down for a moment. I could see that his cock was having small spasms and leaking as well.

With little grace and a few seconds of anxiety, I maneuvered myself so that I was kneeling on the kitchen counter with my back to him. I licked two fingers, then reached under and stuck them both up my ass. When they were in as far as the position would allow I started a slow fuck of my own, grinding onto my fingers like they were his cock. I looked over my shoulder and coyly watched him watching me.

He continued to fuck his ass with his long finger and his cock looked as if it would burst, then he lifted both his legs up into the air and inserted a second long finger. This was all he needed. His cock shot and he leaned into it. He was almost able to put it in his mouth! He shot again and again all over his face, each time opening his mouth and sticking out his tongue.

I pulled my fingers from my ass, turned back around, and sat back down watching him in amazement. Though I knew I couldn't reach it, I dipped my head to receive my own offering and was rewarded with a strong mouthful of hot sperm. I beat it with purpose. My cock seemed to shoot its contents in slow motion up onto my open lips and outstretched tongue.

***

It's 6:45. I'm in my kitchen ready for Blue. I've brushed my teeth and inserted my contacts. I've even fed Cat. I'm wide awake, and ready. Boy, am I ready!

Blue hasn't appeared yet. I'm smoking and feeling

far too anxious. It's okay I rationalize. A guy can't have this much luck every day. Maybe he overslept. Maybe he met someone else and is still in bed. No, he'll show. I'll just start without him. I pull off my boxers and angrily fuck my cock in frustration. I stop when my doorbell rings.

My doorbell?

I run to the door and my heart stops when I look out the peephole. It's Blue. He's wearing jeans, no shirt or shoes. I fumble with the locks and nearly knock myself in the head as I open the door. I stand there naked face-to-face with the man I have had sex with every morning this last week. He smiles.

I'm speechless. He reaches out and wraps his long fingers around my rock-hard cock.

"Morning. Make me some coffee?"

I pull him into my apartment. Well, I back up and my cock pulls him into the apartment.

"I'm a, well..." I stammer as he kneels in front of me. He wraps both his hands around my fat cock. "Oh…" Oh my god. "Oh my…"

I lean over him and close the door just as I feel his mouth make contact.

The slump is over. My dry spell has ended.

## THAT GRIN

Passive/aggressive or depressive tendencies? No. Please! Feelings of self-pity? Low self-esteem? No. No, not at all. My father's fault? No. I doubt it. You think?

Childhood incident?

Maybe.

I remember my Uncle Ron holding me down and tickling me. I hated it. At the time I hated him. I was five or six when he started. It felt so good and so bad all at the same time. I had no control. He was larger, stronger, and more powerful than I was. He was an adult. I didn't understand why he was torturing me, why he was enjoying it so much.

Why was he enjoying it so much?

He was evil.

He had this wild grin once he started working me over. It scared me. And he'd keep grinning until he had me so wired I'd pee myself. Then—usually—he'd stop. He'd timidly rub the top of my head and call me a "good sport."

Would that cause it? Well...

And then there was Roger. God, I thought Roger was so cool. He wore hip-hugger jeans, had a shag haircut, and looked a little like David Cassidy even though it was years after *The Partridge Family*. He was a couple years older than me at 15 and I never understood why he was my friend. But I never questioned it. Never asked him.

He was too cool.

He would spend the night at my house sometimes and we would stay up all night watching scary Hammer Films, like *The Curse of the Werewolf* and *The Kiss of the Vampire*, and laughing. He liked to wrestle. He'd pin me down and make me say "uncle" or "I'm a fag" or "I like to suck dick." And I would. I'd say "I like to suck dick, Roger" even though I hadn't ever thought about what sucking dick really meant. I never thought anything about it. It was fun. He was cool. And I really liked him. I enjoyed the attention he gave me and got hard when he would pin me down even though I didn't understand why.

Then this one time he stripped off all his clothes and started jumping up and down on my bed. I didn't know what to do. He was hard, and his dick was so big. I couldn't believe it. Roger was naked...and hard...in my bedroom.

"Come on, get naked!"

I was stunned, confused, frozen. "I ah—"

"It's fun," he stated simply as he wagged his hardness back and forth at me.

"No, I...ah—"

And he jumped more and his dick bounced up and down making smacking sounds on his stomach...

"YEAHHHHHHHHHH!"

Slap.

"YEAHHHHHHHHHH!"

Slap.

"YEAHHHHHHHHHH!"

Slap.

He stopped. And watched his dick as he stroked himself a few more times. And then he grinned at me. And my heart stopped.

Roger tackled me roughly to the ground. His huge grin confused me. That same grin, only at the time I couldn't make the connection. His hard dick grinding into me confused me even more. Then it happened. He started tickling my sides.

"I...oh, god...no, STOP!" It hurt. Oh, it hurt. It hurt so bad. "Ah ha, hehehe...no, oh god Roger, NO!" Oh, it felt good. It felt so good.

But he didn't. He didn't stop. And I laughed.

"He hehehe OH NO! ah hehehe..."

And he tickled my sides and stomach harder. And he pinned me down with his body, his hard dick pressing against my leg, his breath hot on my face. And he tickled me more. And I laughed until I cried. And I cried and cried. And he grinned and came on my leg.

At least I didn't pee.

And we never talked about it. We never mentioned it.

Would that have caused it?

Maybe...just maybe.

When I was 23, I met Sean. By then I was fully aware what to do when a man with a hard dick was in my bedroom. I had had my share of dick sucking by 23. I had been fucked more than a few times too. But I'd never been tied up. Hesitant at first, I was Sean's once I saw him without his underwear. He had quite possibly the most beautiful, and probably the largest, dick I had ever seen. I let him tie my arms to the bedposts.

"Sure, baby. Tie me up. Just no funny stuff, huh? But you can fuck me, okay?"

But he didn't...not at first. No. First he gave me the real thing: my first taste of what real tickling is.

Is that what caused it? Yes, maybe. But, I can safely say that that was the turning point for me.

He started by lightly rubbing his fingertips up and down the arches of my very tender and sensitive feet. I thought I would come instantly. I didn't, but he did see my dick's reaction. It gave him permission. And he grinned.

Now I knew what the grin was and I recognized it. I cried out "OH NO OH NO OH NO" loudly. More from fear than as a directive. And he kept it up, softly flicking his fingertips across my feet. When he started making sweeps of his tongue over the bottoms of my toes, while still fingering my soles, I was unsure I would survive. I was going to die. Yes. Yes, yes, yes. Right here, now. I was going to die while being tied up and tortured by this beautiful, beautiful man. Then he took my right big toe in his mouth, and reached up with one arm and very, very gently brushed a fingertip across my balls, then my asshole.

"AAAAAAAAAAAAAAH...haha...ah, ha ha ha..."

And I came. I shot harder than I'd ever before. Then he started on the rest of my body. By the time he fucked me I had absolutely no control of my body or my mind. And he did fuck me, hard and without mercy, never once giving up the control he won over me with the hellish sensation of his fingers upon my skin.

I fell in love.

At least for a couple months. Until I met Sean's ex-lover Bill, and we got naked. He brought feathers and insisted on strapping both my arms and legs to the bedposts. Bill tortured me nonstop for two weeks. It was the perfect balance of heaven and hell. Then he disappeared and I never heard from him again.

Since Bill, I've been a total tickle pig. I'm a complete bottom — willing to take any tickle punishment, any amount of pleasure/pain, anything from anyone. I need to see that evil grin, to feel the thing I once feared most. What I still fear but now can't live without. I want to lose all control, or rather, to have the control taken from me.

Sometimes I have fantasies of going out to the baths and begging them to tie me down, spread me wide, secure me. It'll be a gang-bang. As many as 10 guys on me, in me, at once. I don't care. I don't care if I have one in each end, and if they come all over me or pee on me. They can, and often do, in my fantasies. As long as I'm tied down and at least one of them is tickling me or licking my feet they can do anything they want.

I want, desire, need, to experience that moment, that moment when adrenaline kicks in, when all else fades but the intense focused sensation of the tickle. That sweet, sweet torture that starts with the skin but soon encompasses my entire being. The pain. The pleasure. That one moment of perfect focus when I know, just know, that another second of it might kill me.

Will I die, or just go insane?

Sometimes it feels so good/bad I seriously think it will kill me. But it never does. I just ride it.

And the guys. I really don't know most of them anymore; they're just nameless men from ads or chatrooms or bars. Most of the men I meet or fuck don't want me for long. They always want something new. Eventually.

But I've haven't given up on relationships. I'm still hoping to meet the perfect man. The man who will never tire, never want to stop tickling me. And if I find him, it just might kill me. But I'm willing to take that chance. It will be worth it.

I don't know who he'll be or what he'll look like, but he'll have my Uncle Ron's evil grin. The one I didn't understand when I was five or six. The one that scared me so much.

That evil grin.

The one I can't live without.

# GOD

I ask him each time we meet if he is absolutely sure, and he answers my question with the same two questions back.

*Have you found God?*
*Are you sure that you are not going to hell?*

The first line of text took three hours to finish. It runs from shoulder to shoulder across his wide smooth back. He has beautiful skin. It was painful; he cried. Solid lettering, thick and bold. It was perfect. He is perfect.

**Know ye not that the unrighteous**
**shall not inherit the kingdom of God?**

The rest of the text I broke up in several sessions, each taking about the same amount of time, but I worked slower, methodically. The lettering now covers his entire back, wrapping over his finely muscled form like medieval calligraphy.

After the first session, he requested I restrain his arms. I bought soft rawhide strips and bound him face down, wrists firm to each side of the worktable.

**Be not deceived: neither fornicators, nor idolaters,**
**nor adulterers, nor effeminate, nor abusers**
**of themselves with mankind, nor thieves,**

I let the needles dig deeper, draw blood, stain. He learned to enjoy the burn, to ride the pain the gun caused. He cried out as I worked but never moved. I lettered with patience, care. I worked with a hard-on the entire time. So did he.

*Have you found God?*
*Are you sure that you are not going to hell?*

**nor covetous, nor drunkards,**
**nor revilers, nor extortioners,**
**shall inherit**
**the kingdom**
**of**

His skin is warm and salty. I run my tongue across each raised letter and syllable, each newly inked word, and with each lick receive the reward of his moan. I follow the entire passage with my eyes closed, seeing the words in my brain, reading with my tongue.

Tonight was quick. I inked the final letters. One on each of his toned, hairless — once I had shaved them clean — ass cheeks.

*Have you found God?*
*Are you 100% sure that you are not going to hell?*

**G   D**

I taste blood, ink. I taste his lust. I taste sin. I plunge my tongue into his ass, oblivious to anything else, my passion ignited, my masterpiece finished. I growl like a lion over freshly killed prey. I devour with a hunger I've never felt, one that surpasses any before. My fingers graze over his back, comprehending, as if it is written in Braille. He is unable to move with his wrists restrained but pushes back against me, bucking, his thick cock jutting out stiff and wild from beneath. I grab his cock and pull on its slippery skin. He comes loudly and I feel him constrict around my tongue.

When I come up for air, the magic has happened. His asshole is fully dilated and ready, an open **O**, pink and wet. I lick him from my lips as I unzip. I climb onto the table and mount the man who has made himself my canvas, sliding my cock fully into **GOD** with one swift hard thrust.

*Have you found God?*
*Are you sure that you are not going to hell?*

# LOVE

He stands with his smooth back to me. His legs are firm under him, feet secure on the hardwood floor, arms stretched out, his large hands flat on the edge of the table.

*Beautiful.*

His skin is shiny. He is taller then me, his shoulders wide, neck and arms strong, waist small. His round ass cheeks are red from the slaps I gave them when he first stripped down, my emotions taking control immediately. His thighs are muscled, feet long. He is strength in perfection, willing to give up control to another with calm and trust.

*Grateful.*

I walk up and grab his ass cheeks pulling them apart to expose the hairy pucker. I want to kneel and lap at it with my tongue and I groan, letting the sight ignite my desire. I smell it and reach around to grab his cock jerking the foreskin while forcing him against the table with my weight. I push his head and shoulders until flat on the tabletop and his weight lifted forward. I quickly place the plastic bag over his head and pull the edges tight around his throat making a handle as I grab my slippery cock and force it up into his ass with one swift shove.

*Desire.*

He gives little resistance as I pull the full length out and force it back in fiercely, banging against him with all my weight and rage. His hole clenches tightly around me and I feel him shove back despite being off balance, his feet barely touching the floor.

I keep a firm grip on the bag as I fuck him hard and fast. I know I should be careful not to push him too far but I am quickly out of control and can't think of consequences, only the final release. My heart is pounding wildly and my vision blurs. I'm numb. I grind into him wanting to split him open.

*Doubt.*

I pull him upright just as the pressure in my balls tightens to the point of exploding and pull the bag off. I clamp my mouth on his shoulder and bite down, yanking his head back sharply by his long sweaty hair.

He cries out and I feel his ass clench tighter, literally jerking me off with its force. He sprays across the table while the muscles in his ass pump around my convulsing hardness.

*Release.*

He leans his weight against me while his lungs breathe deeply the air they have been denied. I continue to stir in him as I stroke his still-stiff cock. I start to cry. He moans my name softly. I pull his face around and explore his tongue with mine, tasting my tears as they fall down my cheeks.

*Fear.*

I pull my cock out and gently lay him on the table again. I put my mouth to his asshole tasting my sperm mixed with his ass juice. He crawls onto the table and kneels for me, ass lifted up and splayed. I brush my lips on his cheeks.

I slap him hard, as hard as I can. He forces back against my face and I accept. I place my hands on his hips and put my mouth to his hole. It opens up as my tongue slips in and I feed hungrily. Wetness drips down my chin and I place a finger right at the opening to rub along with my tongue. The smell of his ass ignites me again.

*Anger.*

The lights dim abruptly and the ground shifts under my feet. I bite at him, catching hairs with my teeth. I close my eyes to make it stop. I pull my finger out and immediately replace it with two. My cock slaps against the table as I back away dripping both from my chin and cock.

I drink my beer and watch him in silence. He hasn't moved. I step closer to him and press the lip of the bottle against his ripe, swollen ass lips. It slides in and out easily. I smile, then drink the last of it.

*Thirst.*

"Sit on it," I tell him. He shifts to a squatting position and quickly swallows the first half of it. I jerk him by his hair and grab the bottle. "Harder." I kiss him on the back of his neck.

*Tenderness.*

He screams as he forces himself down onto the glass. I turn him around by his hair to face me and pull his head to mine. "Tell me you love me," I say as I grab his cock.

"I luh—" I slap him and grip his cock harder.
I feel the room spinning. I yell, "Say you love me!"

and jerk on his rock-hard meat, sliding the tight skin over the head again and again.

"I love you!" he shouts back as he sits down on the bottle. I see just the bottom inch sticking out. His nipples are hard and I grab them both and pinch. I pull his face to mine and force my tongue into his warm willing mouth. He moans and I feel the tightness pulling on my balls again.

*Pity.*

I growl and grab at the back of his neck, yanking his head down so his chin is against the tabletop. I ejaculate against his lips, then force my cock into his mouth and shoot again. I fuck his mouth, hitting the back of his throat over and over.

I lift him up by his chin and lick his bruised wet lips. I kiss his neck, chest, nipples. I kiss his belly. I take his hardness into my mouth and reach for the bottle. I close my eyes.

*Love.*

I love you too.

# FINGER

I awake abruptly, jumping up as if from a bad dream. My hand grabs at the side of the bathtub. I'm lying inside, naked but for my boxers that are twisted uncomfortably around my balls. I fight the urge to throw up, and wonder whose bathtub I'm in, and why I'm missing most of my clothes.

My head throbs as I try to lift myself up. Once sitting, I contemplate lying back down now that the pain in my head has risen a few notches. I remember having drinks at Harry's bar, yes drinks, and there was a broad. I bought her a drink and told her she looked like Lana Turner. She was...oh, the urge to vomit comes again, and I lean over the edge of the tub and gag. Nothing but bile. Just a little bile.

\*\*\*

"You look like Lana Turner."

"Oh, you sweet talker. You're smooth, aren't you? Buy me a drink, honey. My name's Edie, but I like Lana. Call me Lana."

"Well, Edie, ah, Lana — "

"You know, honey, things aren't always as they seem."

\*\*\*

I lay my head against the cool porcelain and close

my eyes. We'd gone back to her apartment for a nightcap. This must be her apartment, but where was she? She was beautiful...I think. I have a foggy memory of her sitting on the edge of the bed, rolling down her stockings...yes, beautiful. That's the last thing I can remember.

\*\*\*

*"Damn, Lana, You're beautiful."*

*She puts an old record on the turntable, then sits on the edge of the bed seducing me with her eyes as she slowly peels the stockings down her long smooth legs. With a curling finger she signals for me to join her. I sit my drink on the bedside table and walk to her – my cock throbbing against the inside of my now too tight pants – in response to her invitation.*

*"You know, baby, I think I owe you some payback for all the sweet talk and the drinks."*

*She licks her ruby red lips with her tongue as she slowly unbuckles my belt, unzips me, and frees my anxious member. I moan in disbelief at my luck as Lana wraps her mouth around my hard cock and Johnny Cash sings how it burns, burns, burns...*

\*\*\*

Okay, no time like the present, I think. I stand up and step out of the bathtub I've made a bed. My legs feel as if they're having a hard time supporting my weight. I step over my puddle of bile and lean against the sink. My reflection scares me. I have bruises all over my cheeks and my right eye is swollen shut. Shit! I've got to remember what happened after I nailed the broad.

I shuffle to the toilet, lift the seat, and piss for what seems like an unusually long time. My balls feel heavy and ache. I look around the dingy bathroom, flick off the last couple drips of urine, and flush.

There's no medicine cabinet, just a cracked mirror held onto the wall with nails. One after another I open the drawers below the sink in search of aspirin. Finding none,

I decide what I really need is more of what got me here. A good shot or two of bourbon, and if I can find my lady friend maybe a little more loving. An explanation would help.

I grab some toilet paper and blow my nose hard, ratcheting the pain in my head even higher. I toss it towards the trash can, but miss. When I pick it up and toss it again at the target, I see it. A finger.

A finger!

There's a fucking finger wrapped in bloody toilet paper in the trash can!

Panicking, I back up and try to catch my breath before I scream. What happened last night? I sit down on the edge of the tub and start to cry. What fucking happened? I check to make sure all my fingers are still attached, then rest my head in my hands and stare at my feet on the cold white tile of the bathroom.

I had drinks at Harry's. I make friends with a beautiful babe who I share more drinks with. She invites me back to her apartment for a nightcap, we hit it off, I bang her, maybe, and...then what?

\*\*\*

*"Oh, careful Lana! You gotta slow down or you're gonna make me explode. Damn girl!"*

*I pull myself from her mouth with a pop and back up. I'm standing in the middle of her bedroom with my cock bouncing up and down ready to shoot, my pants in a wad at my ankles.*

*She kneels at the edge of the bed, reaches back and unzips her red velvet dress. It falls from her shoulders and she catches it, teasing me, slowly uncovering her lovely small breasts one at a time. I let out a growl, and decide to get ready for the fuck of my life!*

*I trip over my own feet getting to the chair, and settle for the carpeted floor, where I fumble with my shoelaces.*

*"You know, baby, sometimes what you least expect can be exactly what you want the most."*

*Lana stretches out those long legs and gingerly steps off the bed. She takes a deep breath and lets the dress fall. My eyes nearly pop from my head as it billows in slow motion down to her feet. Her tiny nipples harden as she steps out of her black lace panties, one smooth leg at a time, and her thick red cock — red as the dress at her feet, as red as the lipstick from her lips now smeared on my own cock — bounces free.*

\*\*\*

I suddenly remember her boyfriend storming into the room, and he was pissed. He started yelling at her, calling her a cunt, and she was bawling like a baby. He kept shaking his finger at her, his ring finger. His ring finger! I run to the trash can and look in at the finger.

Yes, the finger has a ring still intact. Holy Jesus, have I done it now! If I could just piece a little more together to know how the husband lost the finger. I stand, go to the sink and turn on the water. I splash my face, and swish my mouth out. I don't dry off, just run my hands through my hair, and stare at my face. The skin beneath my eyes is swollen and blood vessels blossom across my nose and cheeks. I look tired. So tired. And scared.

I decide to be brave.

\*\*\*

*"Surprise!"*

*I am speechless. I've gotten in some trouble with drink in the past, but this definitely takes the cake. Oh, but is she lovely. I slowly stroke my cock as the truth sinks in.*

*The front door bangs shut, and I don't even have time to react before the heavy stomping footsteps bring a very large, very angry man into the room. Shit, I still have my pants wrapped around my ankles!*

*His face is red with rage — as red as Lana's thick cock, as red as the dress at Lana's feet, as red as the lipstick from Lana's lips now smeared on my own cock. He looks like he's going to explode!*

> *"You slut! You fucking cunt! Who is this faggot?"*
> *Faggot? "You know Lana, I think – "*
> *"Lana? Edie, you cunt!"*

*He takes three quick steps past me and slaps Lana hard across her cheek, knocking her down onto the bed. Blood spurts from her nose and open mouth and she looks up at him like a cornered animal.*

*He turns back to me and lunges. I try to get up but my pants trip me again, putting my face just where I assume he wants it, right in line with the steel toe of his big boot.*

*Lana is sobbing, half her body hanging off the bed, black mascara tears mixing with the blood, her shriveled cock laying limp against one leg. He storms out of the room after kicking me again, this time right in my balls. My senses all scream at the same time, and I curl into a fetal position.*

*He returns with what look to be gardening shears, and I start screaming bloody murder.*

> *"Not you, faggot! Shut up! Edie, I'm tired of this! I'm so fucking tired! Why do you do this to me? Why do you always do this to me? I love you so much – "*

*The shot makes me jump up and back, and I have just enough time to see him fall to his knees before Lana takes aim and fires her gun at him again, his chest exploding, covering me in thick red viscera. And I pass out.*

\*\*\*

Be brave!

If I get out of this mess, I promise to lay off the drink for a while. God, please, let them both be alive!

I open the door, and on very shaky legs, go in search of Lana and her fingerless boyfriend.

## WALKING OLIVE

I guess I should feel guilty. I mean he is a client and all. But what can I say? Jack has been driving me crazy. I love him. And Bea, my psychic, did tell me that love would be in the picture in the very near future. She couldn't say when, but she did say he had a dog. I know, just know, that it's Jack. We haven't met yet, but I know he's the one.

Every day at 12:15, or as close as I can manage, I visit his house and walk his dog. I walk dogs. I'm a dog walker. Actually I'm an author. I write pornography. But smut don't pay the bills. Not yet anyway. So, I walk dogs during the week. I put on my smartest slacks and most sensible walking shoes, a sweater and hat when necessary, my sunglasses, and strut with the little pooches for 16 minutes or so each, five times a week. Picking up crap ain't that bad as long as you maintain your dignity and hold your nose and make sure there aren't any holes in the bag.

Anyway...oh, hold on. *Good girl, Olive. Good girl!* Olive is a very sweet miniature poodle trapped in a fat little beagle's body. Sometimes you just can't control what body you were given. I know that! *Good God, girl! What did you eat?* Well, picking up crap isn't usually that bad. Dignity, Robbie, dignity!

Where was I? You would think I'm all drugged out the way I zone out sometimes. But I'm not. This girl doesn't put anything unhealthy into her shrine. Yesterday, I was dropping off letters at a mailbox before I started my rounds and it happened. There I was on the corner of Clark and Foster in my new smokin' kelly green leisure slacks that zip up the side and my burnt orange corduroy jacket. Sure, I was wearing a blond fall wig, but sometimes you just get the urge. And it happens: I start thinking about visiting Jack's house. It's so damned tasteful and homey. He always has soothing classical music playing for his dog Jake. I'm sure that's why Jake is so smart. He's a Border collie. He's a major soccer fan — Jack, not Jake — but I guess Jake might be as well, with posters of soccer stars and sports magazines all over the place. So, I'm on the corner ready to cross Clark Street and I started daydreaming about him.

I'd be his perfect bottom. He could fuck me all night long. And I'd say, *Oh yes, Daddy Jack! Fuck me, Jock Daddy!* Unless, of course, he's a bottom. He might be. You think? But he's so butch. He could be my butch bottom! And I, his femme top.

I'd say, *Suck my dick, Jack!* And he would. And I'd hold his head firmly, admiring my new French manicure, while plunging my surprisingly long and perfectly shaped cock in and out of his eager mouth. Oh, the pleasure of his lips and tongue! Oh the pleasure of hearing him slurp. I'd make him gag on it and call him my bitch. I could do that! *Bitch! Deep throat it! You want some mansnot! Make me cum, bitch!* Then I'd pull out and make him get on all fours. I'd fuck him. I'd show my butch bottom who's in charge. I'd fuck him hard! I'd fuck him…

And this wench pulls right up to me and honks, then starts screaming something at me. Guess I was a bit too close to the curb and she thought I was gonna walk in front of her. I snap out of it and look at my watch. Lord help me, I'd been standing there for 15 minutes.

She honked again, and I screamed, *Girl get off my back!* and she yelled, *Wake up!* And I screamed, *Girl!* And she yelled, *Faggot!* Lord, one of these days I probably will walk out in front of a car. *Faggot?! Hey now…* but she'd pulled off. I couldn't help but laugh. That was until I looked down and saw that my little daydream had left me with a wet spot. No problem, it'll dry. They're perma-press!

You can't imagine how long I've been waiting to see inside Jack's bedroom. He writes me these wonderful notes every morning. He takes such good care of his home, and Jake, and his notes are so lovely:

> *Hi, Robbie!*
> *Everything is OK here!*
> *Have a great walk!*
> *Thanks, Jack*

He's a client and there are rules. I've looked through his kitchen, all of his living room and dining room, and his books, his mail, and his bathroom has given me miles of fantasies. But I won't open closed doors. Unfortunately, his bedroom is always closed. But today…Jackpot! I quickly took care of Jake and we did our walk thing — only shorter. I needed to touch some of his stuff, to find out what surprises my man's bedroom held.

Not that I expected a den of sin, with a sling, and oodles of dildoes, vibrators, and flavored sex lube everywhere, still I was a bit disappointed. Just a bed, a dresser, and piles and piles of clothes and shoes all over the floor. Okay, so he's not tidy. That's all right. I'll do the laundry for my man.

And I'll admit his shoes were a bit smaller than I expected — size 9. He's a jock. I expected large feet. Just as I imagine huge strong thighs that'll just about kill me when he tightens them around my head while I'm dining on his huge fat cock and fondling his weighty manballs.

Of course I had to do it: lay down on his rumpled bed and stretch out. I could smell him. *Oh god, Jack, I love you so much. If I could, I'd have your baby.* I'm rolling in ecstasy. I'm so horny. I have to have him! I kick off my shoes. All right, I'll be just a little late for Olive's walk. I clutch at the bedsheets imagining his weight full on me, his tongue in my ear, his stiff cock grinding against mine, then I feel it. Hello. What's this?

At first I think it's just underwear, then realize it's

a jock. Jackpot again! Oh god, I think, I've died and gone to heaven. I pull it to my face and breathe deep. Lord have mercy! This baby's nice and dirty. Unable to control myself, but knowing that I have only a few minutes before I have to leave for Olive, I unzip my slacks and yank my extremely hard cock from its satin confinement.

*You want me to fuck you good, Robbie? Give me some of that sweet manpussy, baby!*

*Oh, yes, Jack! Yes, sir! Yes! Fuck me, stud. Give me that big cock! Ahhhhh…I love you, Jack. I've waited for this so long…*

*I love you too, Robbie. I love you!*

And Jack, my true love, my man, my soccer stud, slides all eight and a half thick inches of his cock swiftly into my tight ass. Oh the joy! Oh the pleasure! Oh, the…

I squeal and cum, shooting hard up and all over myself. Oh, that was good! Oh, what a mess! Thank god I didn't splash his sheets. Jake is wagging his tail and watching with devoted interest from the edge of the bed.

*Don't tell Jack, love. It'll be our little secret. But get used to me being here!*

I waddle to the bathroom with my slacks around my knees trying my best to keep my Jackjuice from spilling on the floor. Look at the time! I fill Jake's water dish, give him a treat, and write Jack a quick love note:

> *Jake and I had a wonderful time today.*
> *1 & 2. Like always!*
> *Fresh H2O and treats.*
> *xxx, Robbie*

I stuff the jock into my jacket pocket. Like I'm going to leave it! Sooner or later Jack and I will meet in person, then fall in love and live happily ever after, but in the meantime, these are keepers!

Oh Lord, zoned again. In my pocket, I squeeze Jack's jock tightly in my fist and come back to the present. I'm sure I'm really behind schedule now.

*Olive girl, you ready to…*

Where'd she go? Shit. How'd she get loose? And I scratched a nail! Fuck! Fuck! Fuck!

*Olive?*

*Fuck!*

*OLIVE!*

# HIS BABY

Sam had never been in love. Never felt its touch or its burn. He felt it now. He felt it in his heart when he looked at Roberto sleeping. An uncontrollable urge to keep him safe and from harm forever. Safe from his past, from the trouble he had gotten himself into, from his quest for both money and love by any means possible.

It's New Year's Eve. Sam and his Baby are in a motel outside Springfield. Not exactly where he had planned. He had wanted to take his Baby to dinner, then home to slow dance and whisper sweet words into his lover's ears. He had chilled expensive champagne, wanting to drink it from his Baby's mouth at the New Year's chime. Instead they were in downstate Illinois and his Baby looked like he'd gotten hit by a truck.

The first time Sam saw Roberto he was driving home from a friend's house after dinner, cautious of the snow that had been falling slowly all evening. Roberto was leaning up against a brick wall on the side of a CURRENCY EXCHANGE, left leg tucked up under him, posing. Many would see him and think that the beautiful man was simply waiting for a bus on this December evening. It was a bus stop, but Sam knew better. The lights from the OPEN 24 HOURS and CHECKS CASHED signs flashed on and off, casting the young man's face in red, and as cars passed, the young man looked into each one with piercing, searching eyes. Waiting for one to slow, then stop and invite him in from the cold and snow. No, this beautiful young man wasn't waiting for a bus; he was working. He was for sale. Sam slowed down and seriously considered picking him up, but as the young man planted both feet down and readied himself to approach Sam's prized fire red 1966 Ford Mustang, the light changed and Sam pulled away. Thankful that he hadn't let the boy in, he drove home.

Sam had had a good life. He had been a successful realtor, made a few very choice investments and retired at 35. Since then, he had enjoyed what time and money allowed him: his house, his dream car, travel, food and wine. But he had never had intimacy. He had only had sex a few times, and that was quite a few years ago. He now had love. He knew it was true love, too. He knew it was real from what had come before. Loneliness. Self-doubt. Pain. Emptiness. He knew it was real because of his increasing willingness to fight his inner demons and accept who he was and what he had to offer, not just to his Baby, but to himself.

And he knew Roberto loved him. It was almost a dream at times. "Who would want me?" had always been his thought at moments of self-hate. Despite the wealth, he was missing what he wanted most: a lover. He was old. He was fat. He was ugly. He was a troll. Who would want a guy like that? Who would want me? No, those were his demons talking, not truth. It was hard to ignore what he had listened to his whole life. But he was trying. Yes, he was older. Yes, he had a belly. Yes, his nose was big and his grey hair thinning. But Roberto said he was handsome. Roberto said his nose was sexy and that his grey hair made him look distinguished. Roberto wanted him, belly and all. His Baby had chosen him.

And he felt it in his gut when his Baby was away. An overwhelming panic that clenched his insides and scared him. He worried his Baby might not return, might not come back to be held, made love to. That he might be dead. Sam knew that Roberto still sold himself, because Roberto had told him so, but he also knew there was more. He would leave for days at a time, then return unwilling to explain where he had been, saying only "But I came home to you, *Papi,* and I'm here now. I love you. I can't live without you. *No puendo vivir sin ti.* You don't want to know where I've been." And he didn't want to know. It scared him.

And he felt it in his cock. And ass. Every time he looked into Roberto's eyes he got hard and his asshole clenched tight.

The second time he saw his Baby, he was having drinks at Gentry's exactly a week after the spoiled attempt to buy the young man. He was alone, but that didn't matter. Sam always went to Gentry's on Tuesdays to listen to his favorite piano man and sing along with the old standards and the occasional show tune. The piano player, Phillip, knew his favorites, and the lovely flirt Marc bartended, and he never had to ask when he needed a drink.

An arm brushed across his, skin lightly touching skin, and reached for a cigarette from Sam's pack of Winston Lights on the table. Long thick fingers pulled one free and Sam admired the hand and the fine hairless wrist before following the hand to the mouth of the intruder who had taken one of his Winstons and the seat next to him.

There he was, the beautiful young man from the bus stop. His Baby flashed him a smile that sealed Sam's fate as he reached for Sam's Ketel One on ice.

"No. I'll get you one."

"Thanks. And for the cigarette too."

"Marc, can you get…ah…"

"Roberto."

"…Roberto a…the same?"

"The same."

"Right away, Sam," Marc said with a wink and a knowing Cheshire Cat smile.

Then his Baby just placed his hand over Sam's, and it was as simple as that. They finished off two drinks each, then left. At Sam's house, they were barely in the door, barely out of their coats, when the young man who would be his Baby held him close for the first time and kissed him. Kissed him deep and long. And Sam could feel the beautiful man's thick cock through his jeans as he pressed himself tight against him.

Roberto had wolfish eyes that could fuck you sweet and hard just by looking at you. But his eyes, his beautiful green gray eyes became even more intense when giving pleasure. They became a window to something deep inside. They pierced right through you and held you captive. They fucked your soul. They fucked Sam's soul.

And when he was deep within the throes of passion his lips sneered up, much like the wolf his eyes presented him as, ready to attack. Hungry. Without mercy. Just focus and a need that he was intent on filling.

They fucked that first night together. Roberto pulled his t-shirt off. His smooth and tawny skin took Sam's breath way. Around his neck and down part of his chest was a tattoo — of *La Chinita*, Our Lady of Chiquinquirá, he would later learn — inked on as if worn on a chain. Sam tried to talk, to ask about the fine tattoo and what it meant, and to ask how much it was going to cost him, but his question was muffled by the piercing eyes.

"Shhhhhhhh…"

"But—"

"Take my clothes off, *Papi. Quitate la ropa.*

"I, ah—"

"*Cogeme.* Fuck me."

They slow-danced their undressing, pulling tight and swaying to an unheard song, then each dispensing of yet another piece of clothing until they both were naked, and Roberto led Sam by his aching hard-on over to the couch and had him sit. His Baby's cock was perfect, certainly longer than most, but not too long. Just thick and hard and slightly curved up. Curved up towards Sam's open mouth and tongue. He licked the bead of precum from the slit before swallowing the perfect cock whole, a moan escaping from both of them. Roberto's came from the sensation of being deep-throated. Sam's came from a long-denied need to be loved by another man.

When Roberto squatted over him, Sam ran his hands over the younger man's smooth shiny skin, down his wide back, over his firm hairless butt, and finally resting them on Roberto's heels.

"*Quiermo sentarme en tu verga.*"

I…what—"

I want to sit on your cock."

Grabbing Sam's head with both hands, Roberto stared deeply into his eyes and lowered his kneeling frame onto the older man's body, taking the squat and very ready cock deep within himself in one smooth motion.

Roberto moved in the next day. Sam now had love and he had his Baby and wanted to do whatever he could to keep him safe and happy. And Roberto had love and his Sam who wanted to keep him happy and safe. But they both knew it was temporary. Sam wouldn't be able to keep him safe for long. It didn't ever work out that way.

Roberto never told Sam of his past. He refused to talk of his home, his family, or his life before Sam, and even though he couldn't understand or speak English very well, he tried hard to use it as much as possible. He tried to never speak Spanish, except in moments of desire or emotion. And he never discussed work.

Here's what Sam thought he knew about Roberto: Roberto was 19. His parents were Colombian. He was born in Colombia but raised in Los Angeles. He sometimes sold his body for money, but not that often. He was working for some bad men. He loved Sam.

Here's what the truth was: Roberto was 16. He was from Colombia. Both parents were dead, killed when he was 10. He had been on the streets since then and selling himself since he was 12. He had been a paid assassin in Colombia and had killed 23 men before getting help from a successful Chicago businessman who brought him to *El Norte* with promises of a better future. He did work for some bad men. Very bad men. The businessman, Krandall, who helped him get to Chicago was now his boss. Roberto ran drugs and fucked for money for him. He did love Sam.

Roberto had wanted to be free of his boss. But he didn't know what to do, how to go about it. He thought of blackmailing him. But that wouldn't work. He thought of just running, which would work, but he wouldn't have any money to run with. Sam had money, but he felt he should too.

He thought he knew how to get the money and get away. He would switch a few bags of money while on his rounds, then pay another kid to beat him up and make it look like he was robbed. Easy.

But it didn't go as planned. He took out most of the money and put it in a locker at the Y. That went fine and he didn't think anyone saw him. He then gave one of Krandall's other "boys" two hundred dollars to fuck up his face. This kid — who called himself Prince Rico — was only more than happy to fuck up his face. He didn't know why he was doing it, but money was money. He didn't care.

But Rico liked to talk. And the gossip spread quickly. It didn't take long for Krandall to hear Rico's version of what he did to Roberto. It also didn't take long for Krandall to do the same to Rico; only he didn't stop with his face. Krandall broke both of Rico's legs. Rico talked. Krandall knew Roberto had the money. He could run on his own, but he loved Sam too much. And they knew where he lived so Sam was in danger, too.

Roberto had crossed Krandall. That left only two options: run or stay and be killed.

"We gotta leave! Now! *Ahora!*" Roberto came storming into the kitchen from the back door and grabbed Sam firmly, making him turn around and face him.

"Baby, what are you —"

"Now, Sam. Now." And his Baby ran out of the kitchen and to the bedroom. He followed him, an alarm sounding off loudly in his head.

"Why now? Why? Baby, what happened! What happened to your face?"

His Baby told him there was no time; that they

had to leave. Leave town. Leave Chicago. Tonight.

And he did what his Baby requested. They left in his Ford Mustang and drove until they hit a snowstorm and couldn't drive any further. They got a room in an otherwise empty motel. Guess it wasn't a hot spot for the holiday.

It's New Year's Eve. Sam and his Baby are in a motel outside Springfield. Not exactly where he had planned. He had wanted to take his Baby to dinner, then home to slow dance and whisper sweet words into his lover's ears. He had chilled expensive champagne, wanting to drink it from his Baby's mouth at the New Year's chime. Instead they were in downstate Illinois and his Baby looked like he'd gotten hit by a truck.

While Sam was out getting some takeout from the diner down the interstate, Roberto searched the drawers for the Bible he knew would be there. Every motel room had one. He found it. It made him feel more secure to clutch it tight to his chest as he prayed over and over to his *La Chinita* to deliver him and his Sam from the trouble he had caused. To save them from certain death if Krandall found him, them. Crossing that kind of man left no alternative other than death.

Roberto fell asleep curled naked on the bed around the Gideons' Bible. On the bed was the Polaroid camera he had begged Sam to buy him for his birthday the week before, and several of the pictures taken with the camera. One was of Roberto wagging his hard-on at Sam. Another was of Sam wrapped in a towel fresh from a bath, all pink and happy, smiling at his Baby. Roberto kept them with him at all times for good luck. The third and final Polaroid was taken as security of a different kind. It was of Krandall and certain member of another crime family coming out of a bar that he had taken when he'd thought of blackmailing him. Not that it would help him now.

Sam came back with fried chicken, mashed potatoes, biscuits, and beer to find his Baby, his Roberto, sprawled out on top of the bed, his hard-on curling back over his smooth tight little belly. Leaving his Baby to dream, Sam tucked the Polaroids — with a huge smile and a hard-on — into the Bible, and set it on the bedside table, then went to wash off the tension and worry in a long shower. A hot shower would help him figure out what they should do next. Then perhaps, after a little chicken, he'd make sweet love with his Roberto. The last love of the year with his Baby, the only man who he had ever loved, the only man who had ever loved him back. Where would they be next year?

Sam didn't hear the door crash open over the running water pounding around his head, nor did he hear the gunshots, or the swoosh of the camera as one of Krandall's men took a picture of the dying boy to take back as proof. When he turned off the water, he did hear the men laughing as they left the room. He wasn't fast enough to see them as they pulled away in their car, wasn't fast enough to save his Baby from the revenge that was destined to happen, wasn't fast enough to keep his Roberto alive.

With his Baby's blood still warm and pooling on the bed, Sam held Roberto tight in his arms and rocked. His Baby was dead. He kissed each of Roberto's eyes, then curled up around Roberto and fell asleep, his hand over the bloody tattoo of *La Chinita*. Two lovers, naked, one in shock and unable to do anything but hold tight, and one dead, his luck gone, as the clock changed years.

## COCK SUCKING IN AMERICA

Last night at Blow Buddies, I sucked the cock of a man whose name may or may not have sounded like Richard Brautigan. I could have been mistaken since the poet Richard Brautigan died many years ago. Not that it has to be the same Richard Brautigan. I'm sure there are plenty. There may even be many in San Francisco alone. So I guess that it's really not that surprising.

He may not even have said Richard Brautigan. It was hot so I had taken my t-shirt off and had it tucked in my back pocket. I was high on mushrooms. It was dark. I was horny. I wasn't really listening because it was hot and I was high on mushrooms and horny in the dark without my t-shirt.

He was leaning back against a wall. He was tall, at least taller than me. He had a good four inches over me and I'm not short. I guess that would mean he was tall. He had a large white moustache that matched his white hair. Like a cowboy's. Like a villain's. A white cowboy villain's moustache. He wore glasses with thick lenses and a very large black fedora hat with a feather in it. He was naked but for his boots, the hat, his glasses, and his white cowboy villain's moustache.

Other than that I couldn't really tell since it was dark. His cock was hard and extremely large and I wanted to put it in my mouth so I reached out and gripped it in my fist.

*Hi. Like your hat. I'm going to suck your beautiful cock,*

I said.

The man whose name may or may not have sounded like Richard Brautigan introduced himself and I got down on my knees and wrapped my other hand around his cock. Like I said, it was large. Two fists wrapped around it and there was still plenty left to put in my mouth.

*You smell like fish,* I somewhat sloppily managed to say while trying to swallow his enormity.

*Trout,* he said.

I looked up from the prize-winning cock in my hands to the white cowboy villain's moustache and large black fedora hat with a feather in it towering over me.

*Whahn?* I asked while trying not to bite down, then pulled my head free to look him in the moustache.

*You said I smell like fish. I do. I smell like trout. I was trout fishing.*

My focus went back to the task at hand, you might say. So I said simply, *Mmmmarhhh...*and wrapped my mouth once again around his large cock and started sucking.

I love sucking cock, and this one was incredible. Despite the smell of fish, er...trout. It was big and juicy, and I used both fists to guide and pump it, while focusing my tongue and lips around the huge head and enormous pisshole.

Sounds of other cocks being sucked surrounded us. The heavy deep moans and gasps, wet slurps and slaps, and occasional gagging sounds only spurred me on.

*I went fishing today.*

*A twelve-inch trout was killed. A rainbow trout named Johnson to be exact.*

*Its life force was taken, not by me, nor by my co-fisherman, a man named Ed with whom I have been fishing since childhood. No. Its life force was shut down, killed dead, by a drink of red wine.*

*Sonoma Valley Cabernet Sauvignon, to be exact.*

*It is against the true nature of life and death for a rainbow trout to die from a drink of Sonoma Valley Cabernet*

Sauvignon.

It is okay for a trout to be caught by a fisherman and die a natural death by drowning in air.

Or, if that said fisherman were a tad more generous and kind, it is okay for a trout to die from having its neck broken before it could drown in air.

This had to be a first. Not sucking a stranger's cock while kneeling at Blow Buddies. No, certainly not that. And certainly not being high on mushrooms while sucking a stranger's cock while kneeling at Blow Buddies, for that is the best way to do it!

But the tale this man, this man whose name may or may not have sounded like Richard Brautigan, was weaving was a first. Does he think it's sexy? Maybe it was and I couldn't tell. It was dark.

It didn't matter. I wanted this cock. I wanted to suck it and make this cock, this two-fisted enormous hard cock, explode. And this cock was attached to this man. So I told myself, I'll just enjoy the story and maybe it will be sexy. Having decided that the story might be sexy, my mouth went crazy with desire.

My pace picked up and I swallowed his cock, or the end of it anyway, with undying focus. Clamping my lips tight and sucking with all my might.

It is okay for that trout to be served up for dinner lightly browned in an oven or fried crisp and served on a bed of long-grain rice with lemon and parsley.

It is okay for that trout to die from pollutants in the lake it has always lived in, or to die from a fungus it has caught in the lake it has always lived in, or to be trapped in a shallow edge when there has been a drought in the lake that it has always lived in and taken in the strong talons of a winged beast to die by being eaten alive.

Or it is even okay for a trout to die of old age with a white beard with its old trout wife next to it.

All of these ways would be okay. But it is not okay for a trout, especially a rainbow trout, to die from a drink of Sonoma Valley Cabernet Sauvignon.

*Mmmm…arhl…mmmufff…*I said in agreement.

*Let me describe how this wrongful deed passed.*

*Today, like every Thursday, I went trout fishing with my friend Ed. Ed is my friend. And we fish.*

*We don't fish for food for dinner. Nor do we fish for the sport of it. No, Ed and I fish because we are friends and that is what friends do.*

*Every Thursday we travel to Lake Del Valle. That is where the trout are. So that is where we fish.*

*Like very Thursday, we set out in our canoe and let ourselves drift on Lake Del Valle as our canoe sees fit. We drink Sonoma Valley Cabernet Sauvignon and drift. When our lines are cast and we do catch a trout, we ask its name, then throw it back in. This way we make new friends. And in this way we also know if we've met this trout before since many trout look alike but not many have the same name.*

*'What is your name, trout?'*

*'Johnson,' the trout said.*

The cock in my mouth, which even when I first began the blow job was clearly one of the biggest I'd ever had the pleasure of meeting face-to-face, was now almost more than I could handle. The cock of the man whose name may or may not have sounded like Richard Brautigan was now a monster whose slippery drooling head banged against the back of my throat with each thrust, causing me to gag. It may have been the mushrooms, or maybe the heat and the mushrooms, or maybe the fact that is was so dark and hot and I was high on mushrooms, but I was having a hard time breathing. Or maybe it was just because he was so big. Or maybe it was his story about trout fishing at Lake Del Valle.

I started using both fists, now sopping wet with precum and saliva, to fuck his monster cock into my mouth, leaving just my lips on the enormous head and pisshole, which at any moment might become large enough to swallow me, and looked up into the general vicinity of the white cowboy villain's moustache and black fedora hat with a feather in it.

In my peripheral vision, I could tell that we were drawing a crowd of cock-sucking enthusiasts, stroking and sucking and moaning along with us. Perhaps they were enjoying the vision of me masterfully strangling the monster cock, or perhaps they were, in fact, enjoying the tale of trout fishing. It didn't matter; I loved an audience. And judging from the cock of the man whose name may or may not have sounded like Richard Brautigan, and the gusto with which he rammed it into me while never missing a beat of his story, so did he.

*Johnson was certainly a beauty. He was twelve inches long and had stripes of many colors running down his sides.*

*'Johnson. Don't believe we've met. This is Richard. I'm Ed,' said Ed.*

*'Are you a rainbow trout, Johnson?' I asked.*

*'Put me back in my lake now, please,' the rainbow trout named Johnson requested.*

*But this is where today took its evil turn against nature. Ed decided he wanted to take Johnson home for dinner. We had never killed a fish while fishing, so we discussed how it should be done.*

*'Don't be cruel. Break its neck so it will die fast,' I suggested.*

*'No, please don't break my neck. I want to grow old and die naturally in my lake home,' said Johnson.*

*'Johnson, please be quiet,' said Ed.*

*'You could just leave it out of the water and it will suffocate,' said I.*

*'I know!' Ed announced. 'Since I am going to take you home for dinner and serve you to my wife and kids, the least I can do is soothe your nerves and dull your pain with a taste of our fine Sonoma Valley Cabernet Sauvignon.'*

*'What about my wife and kids?' the rainbow trout Johnson asked.*

*Then Ed held the poor unfortunate trout up and poured a shot of our fine Sonoma Valley Cabernet Sauvignon down into his mouth.*

*Johnson spasmed, coughed, then died.*

*'He died happy,'* Ed said.
*But I don't think so.*

And with that, the man whose name may or may not have sounded like Richard Brautigan grabbed his giant cock in his own two fists pulled it from my mouth with a pop and jerked. I leaned back and his enormous monster shot onto my chest. Over and over, globs of warm hot monster cum fell onto my neck and chest.

It was raining cum. The room smelled of man sweat, fish, er…trout…and cum…

and…

mayonnaise.

His cum smelled like mayonnaise.

*Mayonnaise,* he proclaimed.

Our audience erupted in applause, as well as what sounded like several other orgasms. I heard *Oh, fuck, yeah* and *Ahhhheeee ohhhh* and one man said *Gawd dammit shit* and I also heard the distinct sound of cum falling and smacking onto cement.

I thanked him and told him I loved his poetry.

*Thank you. I love your poetry,* said I.

He then thanked me.

*Thank you. I love your poetic cock sucking,* said he.

I stood, then wiped the overly excessive amount of cooling mayonnaise off my chest with my t-shirt that had been tucked into my back pocket, tossed the shirt into a trash can on my way out and headed for home.

## BIBLES 10% SALE

My hands are raw and numb as I fumble with your zipper. I kneel, shivering before you under the blizzard white evening sky; my knees hard on the cold snow-carpeted cement; my head turned up as if in prayer. A prayer that your words earlier weren't true.

The snow is falling thick and heavy, wheeling through the light on the street corner. You peel down your jeans and offer your cock to my mouth. I accept it with sadness, devotion, and a deep hunger. Your expression reveals nothing and mine too much.

The air is wet and cold on my face and you are hard as ice in my hand. You are harder and crueler in my mouth. You thrust without mercy and my eyes tear as I give you your final gift and receive mine.

You are so hard and cruel. Don't go.

A lone car is slowly moving toward us up the street — pounding beats of Moby in its warmed interior — and I remember back to when I heard the song last. You had just told me you loved me, and I kissed the jagged scar on your chest, nearly dying from the pain of happiness you'd given me. You came loudly as I licked the deep ridges of your scarred skin and you called me baby.

You said that you loved me.

You shy away with the beats pulling closer, but I draw you back to my mouth. Don't stop. This is all I have now. I need to have you now. You called me baby. You called me your baby.

The car floats by without a notice and you resume thrusting.

Under the blizzard white evening sky, I spill my bitter white love for you on the snow around my knees, and I swallow yours. I wish I could swallow you whole and keep you close. You told me that you no longer loved me as you once did. You no longer loved me.

You no longer love me.

Through my tears, I watch the lights blink on and off in the store window across the street — Bibles 10% Sale/ Merry Christmas/Happy New Year. This is the final gift of the season.

# JOHNNY WAS

Not a day has gone by when I haven't thought about him.

He was some image of beauty, Johnny was. A smile that could kill. That funny space between his front teeth. Every time he flashed that smile at me, I melted. I couldn't stay mad; I could forgive him anything.

Johnny had a perfect body. Trim, strong, compact. Lovely large pierced nipples that were so sensitive he could come from just a few minutes of either soft sweet caressing or my heavy-duty tugging. He had a beautiful long cock and a perfect ass — round and firm with skin as smooth as a baby's — that I both gratefully worshipped and tortured for hours on end.

But I never understood what was going on in his head. He never allowed me to know his thoughts, his past, or what he wanted from his...or our future. Never shared emotions other than his sexual desire and a random "I love you" during orgasm. It's almost like he used me, like I was set up. Like he was just waiting. Like he knew all along how it would end.

I loved him. I could forgive him almost anything. But I will never be able to forgive him for leaving me like he did.

\*\*\*

*David never really understood me. I loved him, which he never seemed to believe, but he was chosen right from the* start to be The One. We weren't destined for a lifetime together, to set up a home or share banking accounts. We were destined for exactly what happened. And I love him more than I have ever loved another for what he gave me. The only thing anyone ever gave me that truly mattered.

***

We met in a most bizarre way, Johnny and I.

I was leaving work late and heading down the block by my office, wishing for a stiff drink to wash away the memory of a long day, when I saw him leaning up against my little Honda's front hood. As I neared, I felt both fear and excitement bristle through my body. It was dark, but there was enough light from the streetlight. It illuminated him. And he was gorgeous. God, he was gorgeous. Black hair framed his pretty face. His two- or maybe three-day-old beard added even more depth to his already high cheekbones. And his pale blue eyes stared right through me.

And my cock hardened with thoughts of tasting him, of working off the day's frustrations.

I couldn't tell what he was doing. It almost looked like he'd been waiting for me. When I was but ten feet from the car, he stood up and I saw that smile for the first time. He flashed me that smile, and that funny space between his front teeth. I smiled back; how could I resist?

And then he kicked out my front left headlight.

"Fucker!" I yelled and started running towards him.

He bolted quickly down the block and I did my best to keep up, all the while yelling obscenities at him. I'm not sure what I thought I was going to do if I caught him, but I ran anyway.

Only a chance car turning from a cross street gave me the opportunity I needed. He dodged the car, tripped over the curb, and fell hard. And I pounced.

"What the hell was that about?" I screamed as I

grabbed his shoulders and roughly twisted his body onto his back.

"I..."

I held him down with my body and wrapped both hands firmly around his neck. Something had snapped and I was going to get a reasonable answer or hurt him real bad. I might hurt him anyway, the stupid fucker.

"Who the fuck do you think you are doing that to my car?"

"I..."

"Tell me why you did that or I'm going to beat the shit out of you!"

My spit flew out in a shower across his beautiful face as I screamed and pressed my hands tighter around his neck and squeezed. I really wanted to hurt him. That's when I saw his smile the second time and felt his hard cock pressing up against my body.

"I wanted to get your attention."

It worked.

I kissed him firmly on the lips, all anger giving way to desire, white-hot lust, and when he returned my kiss, grabbing me by my hair and holding me tight to him, I knew I was in trouble. I fell from lust into love. God help me, I fell in love.

\*\*\*

*He thought I did it because I was hurt by what he said. Not true. He thought it was his fault. It wasn't. The time was right and the doorway was finally open: I had him upset enough that I could take advantage of the moment and finally escape. Poor sweet David. I didn't want to hurt him, but I needed to do it. He just never understood me; I needed to do it. And I needed him to do it for me.*

\*\*\*

The fight was dumb. About nothing really, but it

ended up getting out of hand. I said some stupid mean things about him being an emotional cripple and that he didn't deserve me. He did what he always had done during the six months we'd been fucking when confronted by my anger, or any emotion for that matter: he just smiled. But tonight it pissed me off and I slapped him hard across the face and told him it was over.

"It's over, asshole! No more. I can't play these games any more!"

He started crying and his tears burned deep into my heart. I should have known better than to try and make up. Should have known better than to engage in the play we so often did. It was foolish to play when I was mad.

*** 

"Baby, are you okay? Does it feel good?"

I'd found that talk was important in the play I enjoyed so much. The play I needed so much. Sex was where I let it all out: all the loss of control I felt in my life every single day was overcome by taking that control back. I sometimes pushed too much, losing touch with reality in the moment. Communication was key so that I knew when our playing was enough and when it had become too much, because sometimes I couldn't stop unless told to. This was especially true with Johnny. Our sex had become more and more dangerous with time.

He encouraged me, it. Said he needed it. And he told me he knew I needed it, which was true.

*** 

*I trained him well for the purpose he was meant to serve. Death had always escaped me — or rather — I had always escaped it. I wasn't afraid of it, just unable to follow through with crossing over. But...when I saw David — at a sex-play party where he totally beat the shit out of some boy — but looked so guilty afterwards — I knew he would be the one to help me. I knew he would help me as no other had.*

*He didn't see me that night. I tracked him down. I watched him and learned his schedule. I arranged our first meeting and I made him fall in love with me. And I trained him to be my assassin. He was perfect.*

\*\*\*

Johnny was on his back and his arms were roped to the corner posts of my bed. His beautiful strong legs were over my shoulders and my cock was buried deep within his ass, his sweet hairless ass that willingly took so much abuse from me. Both of my hands were firmly circling his delicate neck and I was beginning to cut off his air supply by pressing my thumbs down firmly across his windpipe.

"Baby, are you okay? Does it feel good?"

"Yes. Come on! Do it! Fuck me...damn it, fuck me hard!"

"Let me know..."

"Shhhh...just fuck me, David. Shut the fuck up and do it."

And I did. Sweat dripped down my body and pooled on his chest and stomach as I continued pounding and then even more deeply into his gut with all my energy. Grinding my length into his tight ass, letting my passion take over. He would never look me in the eyes while I fucked him. Never give me any indication through his face of either pain or pleasure when I applied pressure to his windpipe. It was so risky. I had to watch his coloring and try to tell from his body's tenseness when I needed to stop.

But then he would surface from death's haze, breathing deep, and I would feel his ass clamp down around my cock, and he would look deep into my eyes. And I would mistake it for love. I would mistake his body's natural reactions for the emotions I so wanted and needed. And I would come hard as I looked into those eyes, so hard, then melt into his arms and hold him tight.

We had a rhythm after doing it for months; I knew just how far I could push him. He wanted to get right to the edge, taunting death, as he liked to say. Should I have known it would end as it did?

\*\*\*

*Yes, baby. Tonight is it. I feel it. Come on. I need you now more than ever. Don't disappoint me, David. You'll forgive me in time. Fuck me. Fuck me hard. Hurt me. Kill me. Kill me, lover. I want to feel death as you come. Kill me now.*

\*\*\*

I knew just how long I could deprive him of air to give him the rush he so desired. Then I would let go with both hands to allow him to resurface from death's embrace. His eyes would meet mine and my hard cock would pound once more with such fierceness I'd scream and then erupt as his ass clenched tight around me.

I thought I knew just how long, how hard to strangle to prolong his desire, my passion, his death, my orgasm. My control. I thought I was in control.

But, something wasn't right. He didn't resurface. He didn't come back. I had gone too far. My Johnny left me. He left me as I emptied myself and I knew it was too late to stop either of us.

I couldn't stop.

\*\*\*

*Thank you, David, my love. Don't be angry with me. My last sensation was of your cum pulsing into my ass and I feel it still. I love you so much. I know you don't understand, but I do love you. Thank you. It was perfect.*

\*\*\*

Johnny died. He died with that damn smile on his face and my cock deep in his ass. But I won't forgive him. This time the smile didn't work. He died from my hands. And to my death it's going to haunt me.

\*\*\*

I watch the liquid flow through the IV tubes the State Medical Technician has put into each of my restrained arms. First he will feed me the Pentothal to put me to sleep, then the Pavulon will follow in a dose large enough to paralyze my diaphragm and lungs. Then the final drug will be administered. The potassium chloride will induce cardiac arrest, and I will die.

\*\*\*

Not a day has gone by when I haven't thought about him.

And that funny space between his teeth.

# CROPPED

The air is thick with the scent of damp earth from this morning's weekly watering of the jungle of houseplants. Buffy bathes and the bright California Sunday-afternoon sun streams in onto his orange feline body through the bedroom's window.

He stops his grooming for a moment, focusing his gaze up and over the end of the metal bedpost to his humans on the bed, but quickly loses interest in their Sunday games and rolls over to warm his furry stomach in the bright stream of light.

With a hiss the riding crop comes down again on Tony's balls.

*SNAP!*

"So beautiful…"

And then again twice, this time against the underside of Tony's deep red and painfully hard cock.

*SNAP! SNAP!*

"Ah…what an angel. Look at that porn-star dick!"

*SNAP!*

Tony is in his favorite position: on his back in the middle of their queen-size bed, his legs pulled back into an extreme V, ankles cuffed and snugly roped to the corner posts. He's naked except for a pair of socks, still damp from the run they took together earlier. This splayed-wide position leaves his cock and balls available to Shane's administrations and his asshole stretched open and ready for any abuse he's so hoping will come.

*SNAP! SNAP!*

The crop slaps twice on his upper belly just above the spot where his cock points, then grazes up his chest to his nipples, first one and then quickly the other — each adorned with two small plastic clamps — and taps them none too gently, causing a bright flash of pain and an angry yellow light to explode in Tony's vision.

Though completely secured from his ankles, Tony's arms are free. It took some time to get used to the personal restraint he had to show, not instantly cringing and flailing his arms when something happens. But he knows that Shane takes great pleasure in watching his eager bottom writhe under his firm and talented hand, and even greater pleasure — being a true sadist through and through — by the fact that Tony has to control his own arms and hands while being tortured. So Tony learned to let the energy from the endorphins roll out in waves from his arms that lie flat on either side of his body, much like a gymnast uses them for balance, and only occasionally do they even grip at the flannel sheets when the urge to flail them becomes too great. He then stretches out his fingers, letting the release of control and the resulting energy fight any panic.

"Come on, baby. Don't hold back, Tony. You know what I love the most. Make some noise, beautiful man."

Shane's deep brown eyes drill into his.

*SNAP! SNAP! SNAP!* up the inside of his right leg...

"AH...oh oown oown...AEE—"

Then quickly *SNAP! SNAP! SNAP!* down his left.

"AE AE AE...aaaaaaaah...FUCK!"

*SNAP!* sounds the crop on his right ass cheek, then *SNAP!* on his left. Trying his best to breathe deep and full, readying for what is coming, he nonetheless holds his breath and bites down hard on his bottom lip when it does come.

*SNAP! SNAP! SNAP!*

As Shane crops his asshole the endorphin waves

start to roll in earnest. Tony can only focus on specific details: the brilliant red color of the roses on the bedside table Shane had delivered to him this morning along with fresh pumpkin muffins and the Sunday paper; the silver and turquoise of the ring on his lover's wide hand that firmly holds the shiny black riding crop now buzzing with so much psychic energy that Tony swears it almost leaves colorful trails much as if he were doing acid; Shane's full pink lips and brilliant white teeth as he sneers and smiles to show his pure pleasure and enjoyment.

Tony takes a long deep breath. He smells the wet houseplants, the roses, the newsprint from the Sunday paper. He smells Shane, whose body gives off a scent like no other when excited and relieving sadistic urges or delivering pleasure. And he smells himself: his funky sweated feet; his own acidic scent that comes with pain and pleasure; and he smells his own asshole. His own asshole's ripe and consuming scent—though he would never admit to anyone but his lover Shane—that this turns him on immensely.

He tries to lift his ass higher, but the position leaves very little movement capability.

"That's it, love. Who's my ass slut? Come on…tell me. Tell me!"

*SNAP!*

"I am!"

*SNAP!*

"What do you feel?"

His body heats up, every inch of his skin crackling with electricity, his asshole awash in sensations he is unable to clearly describe. And Shane knows he has difficulty defining it, which gives him even more pleasure by asking him to.

"Baby, I need you. Please fuck me. Now. Please…don't make me talk, fuck me, I can't—"

*SNAP!*

Shane lays the crop on the bed next to Tony's head, and dips his face to Tony's aching asshole, lapping and tonguing the hot pucker, and groaning deeply like a hungry beast over its kill. He then floats—or so it seems to Tony from his position—off the bed. He gently picks up Buffy and places him in the hall, closing the door. He then lifts from its hook on the wall the soft leather blindfold and fits it over Tony's head.

And while Buffy whines and meows many hours too early for his dinner outside their bedroom door, Tony hears the familiar sound of the bottle of lube opening, then feels the cool wetness as it's squeezed into his still hot and stinging asshole. All other sensations melt away when he feels his lover's thick cockhead begin to probe; all is now focused on his asshole and Shane's hard cock. And as the cock slides in, slowly but without any hesitation, his vision of the blackness behind the blindfold explodes into bright white.

# FRISCO

My name is Joshua Clark II, Josh to my friends and clients. I volunteer on Fridays at the Brighton Retirement Home, a low-income old-age residency on Nob Hill, donating my time and services to some of the old guys who will end their days living there.

My favorite Friday friend is Manny Freed, also known as Frisco. He's always my first visit. He's 70 years young. His body's not too sound anymore, but his mind is sharp. No known family. Lonely. But quite a character. And an amusing past. I never really know whether I should believe the tales he tells or not, but they're certainly colorful, and he gets so excited when he spins them he lights up.

I'm running late today, thanks to a lengthy call from my mom, and after checking in with my supervisor, Nurse Wretched, I find Frisco in the TV lounge, on the couch, his big feet on the coffee table in front of him, a can of Fresca in one gnarly hand and a More cigarette in the other. His attention is firmly focused on a rap video he is watching, and the More's ash is way too long, just barely holding on, ready to fall into his lap at any moment.

"Frisco!" I scream, probably louder than I should. "I thought you were supposed to cut down on those."

The ash breaks off, bouncing down the front of his robe, then falling between the spots and white hair of his bare legs to the tiled floor, still in one piece.

"Josh, my boy. Glad you came. You're late. Verna here isn't being very sociable today. I can use the company." With that, he pokes his bony fingers and prissy cigarette at the little round lady with blue hair wearing pink chiffon seated in one of the other chairs, also watching the video. She doesn't react to me being there, or to her name being mentioned. "Let's go to my room."

He puts his cigarette out in the ridiculously large and horrid ceramic horoscope ashtray, and I help him to stand up. We slowly walk down the hall, arm in arm, like best friends, or lovers, to his room, him carrying his Fresca, and me with my brown paper bag of gifts and windbreaker.

"Did you know I once knew Andy Warhol?" he asks once we get to his room and sit down in the two chairs at the foot of his bed.

"Why no, Frisco, I didn't."

"Do you know who he is? You might be too young."

He's a big butterball of flattery, that Frisco. I am too young! But should I be insulted that he thinks I don't know my pop and art history?

"Yes, I do," I respond.

"It was through him that I first met Joe Dallesandro. Ever seen any of his films?" He sounds so serious, and he has a very funny look on his face, like extreme gas, or maybe love. He smiles thinly, then takes a sip of his Fresca.

"I have. He's a babe, Frisco. Very foxy. He was in those Warhol flicks *Flesh* and *Trash*, right? I saw them last year at the Castro during Warhol week. Oh, yeah, and *Heat*. I loved *Heat*! Do you really know him?"

"Paul Morrissey? The director? Yes, I knew him."

"No, Joe."

Frisco yawns. His pale blue eyes look tired, watery and red. I glance at the clock on his bedside table: 2:30. Oh, I really am running late today. Too bad. Frisco's usually napping by now, and I should already be onto my next visit down the hall, with Mr. Kasner.

"Frisco, it's past your nap time. Let's get you in bed." His hair is all messed up. I reach over and comb the thinning wisps of white to one side with my fingers, then pad the cowlick down in the back. "There, better."

"I'm not a baby, damn it!" he snaps, then gives me a look that could kill. I give him one right back that lets him know he shouldn't fuck with me. "Fine, help me up then."

I get up and close his door for more privacy, then help to lift him up. We shuffle over to his bedside, and his good mood returns. "Aren't you gonna ask me about Joe Dallesandro, Josh?"

"Sure. Sure, Frisco." I pull the thin cotton robe off his shoulders and lay it down in one of the chairs. I pull back his bed sheet and tap his bed with my palm as an invitation. "How'd you meet him?"

"He was in love with me, actually. We met at the Factory—"

"Here, Frisco..." I interrupt, peeling his baggy undershorts down, helping him sit on the bed, then pulling them off each leg. I put my arm over his shoulders and lay him on his back, lifting each leg up and onto the bed. Frisco is naked except for his dirty stretched out t-shirt and his black socks. "How'd you meet?"

"...you wouldn't know it now, but I was once a good-lookin' guy..."

Unlike the rest of Frisco's body, which has aged and looked as though it was on its last stretch, his cock showed no sign of aging or willingness to slow down. Despite being framed in brittle white hair, it's a beautiful sight to behold: perfectly sculpted, with a smooth pale shaft and thick blue veins and a huge tawny brown mushroom head, and when hard, like now, it's extremely large and impressive. Down right mouth-watering.

I pull two Trojan Magnum XL condoms from my gift bag. I buy them just for Frisco since he's so big. He's worth the extra investment.

"...and once he tasted me, he was hooked. He fell in love with me, Josh, but..."

I quickly walk to the door and slip the lock on, just

in case Nurse Wretched decides to check in on us, then hurry over to his side. His eyes are closed and he is still spinning his yarn like we were having tea together in some bistro. But his cock knows different. It's ready for action.

"…Paul was there and he took movies of Joe and me naked, doin' it right on the couch with Andy watching…"

I open each condom from its foil and roll first one, then another for good measure, *better safe than sorry*'s my motto, over his trembling monster cock. I lean over and lick his hairy balls. He smells really good: a mix of piss and sweat and skin, but sweet, kind of like a baby. I lick the length of his cock. I then grip it firmly in my fist so it stands straight up and swallow as much as I can in one gulp.

"Little Joe…oh, Joe. Yes…"

I suck him hard, giving his cock my undying focus, long full strokes while clamping my lips and tongue as hard around him as I can, using my fist to jerk it at the same time. I'm good at what I do and I know he'll shoot pretty quickly.

"Joe!"

Frisco's hands pull at the back of my head and he bucks against my face. I keep one hand firmly grasping the bottom half of his cock so I won't choke. He's pretty frisky and this baby's a bit too huge to chance it without a handguard.

"Joe! Oh, Joe! I'm going to come!"

And he does, thrusting himself hard up into my mouth. I feel his entire cock convulse, the underside pumping and the head spitting, pumping and spitting, pumping and spitting, spitting come into the tip of Trojan #1.

"JOOOEEEWWW!"

I almost wish he wasn't jimmied so I could taste him. I'm sure it would be an impressive and tasty mouthful. I suckle for another minute, then pull my head free and lay his arms down at his sides.

Frisco is still except for his chest slowly rising and falling. I peel both condoms off and tuck them in the plastic baggie I brought, then back into the gift bag so no one will find them. When I turn back, he's sleeping, a soft snore coming from his damp liver-spotted lips. I grab a baby wipe from the bathroom and dab at his cock, still hard, still beautiful, and hopefully happy enough to hold him until next week, then toss the wipe in his waste bucket.

"Sleep tight, sweetie," I say and kiss him on his cheek. I grab my bag and windbreaker, and pull out the newest copy of *Bound & Gagged* magazine that I've brought for him. I slide it — with two travel packets of Glide lubricant — under his pillow and head as a surprise for later, then pull the bedsheet over his sleeping naked body. Don't want Nurse Wretched to get too excited if she finds him that way!

I check myself in the mirror in his bathroom. I smile and ruffle my hair up a bit. I look good: healthy and happy. Sunshine on my cheeks, bright eyes, and a dazzling Dream Date smile. I'm fortunate. That's why I like to donate my time and talent to others who are in need and lonely, to share what I can.

Blowing a kiss to Frisco, I unlock the door and prop it open, then head down the hall to Mr. Kasner's room. He promised me pictures of his grandchildren, and I promised him a new Bel Ami video to sneak late at night. He won't take too long. He doesn't like to tell many stories, just likes to stick it in and get it over with wham-bam like. But he's sweet. I should be back on schedule then.

Volunteering is such satisfying work.

# DINNER WITH JESUS

I left San Francisco this morning. Victor picked me up at the airport in Madison this afternoon in his beat-up old Ford pickup truck. How butch is that? It had been a direct, though choppy, flight. My nerves were smoothed over by the 20 milligrams of OxyContin that my roommate Miss Vera had given me at the airport. Actually, they were more than smoothed over. I was really high. But I was still on edge. This was crazy: to travel halfway across the country to Spring Green, Wisconsin to pose for a painter I'd never even met. Victor Salgerno.

My websearches of Spring Green had only come up with info about the architect Frank Lloyd Wright, state parks for hiking and rafting, and the notorious serial killer Ed Gein. A few websites later I found out Mr. Gein was from Plainfield — pretty far away from Spring Green. Sure, the murders might have happened five decades ago, but I don't care. There was no way I was going to travel anywhere close to the home base of that sick fucker. Dead or not. He dressed up in the skin of his victims. Damn. How sick is that? Gives me the willies.

But I had seen Victor's work before. He is part of the new wave of American painters, whatever that really means. His work is kinda odd, but good. Sensual. He does these vivid oil portraits. Bright colors. Detailed. Very carnal. Full of trees and ferns with lots of food and rotting fruit and naked posed men.

That's where I come in. My real name's Talvin.

Talvin Chandra. But most know me — those who do know me, that is — as The Persian Prince, even though I'm not. Persian or a prince. My mom's mom was white and her dad was African-American, which in the U.S. means my mom is African-American, and my dad's family was originally from northern India. My fellow schoolmates ignorantly used to shout out I was a JewRab. You know, looks like someone from the Middle East, but you can't quite figure out where exactly. It was rough as a kid, but I've grown into it quite well. I'm very pleased with the genes I was given.

I'm an actor. Well, that's what they call it: acting. I'm best described as an adult performer. I've made 10 films. My specialty is foot fetish. As the bottom. I'm a bottom through and through, and my pretty-boy JewRab face, fat dick, what are considered by many to be big beautiful feet, and my willingness and capacity to withstand both extreme tickling and ass poundings by big-cocked co-stars, have helped create a loyal following in such films as *The Persian Prince*, *Return of the Prince*, *Torture the Prince*, and *Foot Fuck* parts *I*, *II*, and *III*.

I didn't set out to be an adult-film actor. I went to the University of California at Berkeley and was on my way to a master's in Twentieth-Century Middle Eastern Literature. A lot of good that would have done me nowadays unless I wanted to teach. Which I had planned to. But my attention span and lack of money caught up with me. The details aren't really important. I was broke. I agreed to do a porno film with a friend for some bucks. They liked it. I liked it. I found it exciting to do it with bright lights and a camera, so I did another. It's funny how quick my life plans all changed. Bye, bye U.C. Berkeley. I'm now so popular I have a personal Persian Prince pay website that gets about 2,500 hits a day.

That's where Victor found me. He contacted me through my website and well, here I am. Three week's work, top dollar. Supposedly without any catches, no complications, just posing. We'll see about that. He's probably a big perv. But I'm a model, not a hooker, and I won't do him unless he's hot. My contract with Spread Eagle Studios states that all work go through them — including the money from any such work — but I don't want to share. I just won't tell them. They think I'm on vacation with my mother.

\*\*\*

It's about an hour's drive from the airport to Victor's house so I just kick off my shoes, wiggle my porn-star toes, and relax. We drive with the windows down. It's 85 out, hot and muggy, but the breeze is nice.

Victor slips in a CD of *Rubber Soul* and I start to feel more comfortable. Could be the OxyContin since it's time-released. It feels great to be in the country, around less people and a lot of trees. It even smells green. San Francisco is a fun city but there aren't many trees. And too many people. It's best described as a medieval city, where people piss and shit in the streets and the sick and crazy roam free. I need a little time away, even if it is work.

I love the Beatles. I love this album. I lean back, enjoying the music, and smile at the artist I will live with for the next couple weeks.

Victor is a big man. His bulk takes up the entire half of the front seat. He's wearing cut-offs and a red t-shirt. The t-shirt is very tight, stretched over his large chest and even larger belly, just barely covering the mound. His legs are thick, tanned dark, and hairy. Very thick, but clearly muscled. Solid. Sexy. I feel a rustle of excitement in my dick as I trace their shape with my eyes.

He's handsome, what some would call distinguished, but I would just call Daddy. He has a great profile, all nose and thick lips, with shiny, clean, tanned skin, and his short hair, bushy eyebrows, and full beard are edging towards the salt end of salt-and-pepper. I didn't know Daddy Claus lived in Wisconsin. Yummy. I softly rub my dick — which is getting harder by the minute —

though my jeans. I wonder what adventures are ahead.

A scar runs from his nose to his right cheekbone. I want to touch it. To run my lips and tongue over the groove. To taste it.

"Where did you get the scar, Victor?"

"My ex-wife. She was a mean bitch." He laughs loudly and throws me a wicked grin. Funny. I had thought he was gay since he found me through the site. My boner softens a bit.

I laugh with him. "Oh?"

"No, actually Sheila wasn't a bitch. She was just high-strung. And jealous."

"Jealous of what?"

"My work mostly. She didn't seem to mind that my work was sensual or that I used live models. No, she was jealous that so much of my time was spent doing it. And the passion. My passion is my painting. Poor girl just couldn't compete."

"Is that why she's now an ex?"

"Yeah, pretty much. One morning I woke up. No, actually it was afternoon. I quite often work all night on a canvas then sleep in. That afternoon I awoke and she was packing.

"'Where are you off to Sheila?'

"'I'm not sure you would have noticed me gone, Vic.'

"'Come on, Sheila, don't—'

"'I'm going to Tampa to visit mother—'

"'But you hate your mother—'

"'I need a break from this heat—'

"'Heat? It's 95 in Tampa—'

"'From here, Victor. From here.'

"'Oh.'

"'And you.'

"And she left. She went to Florida. She filed for divorce about a month later. I didn't fight it. We both were ready for the next phase that life had to offer."

What could I say? I nodded and watched the

scenery of green out the window. Damn, it smelled nice here.

"That's too bad."

"No, it's fine, Talvin. Fine."

"Call me Tal."

"Okay, Tal. We're both much happier apart."

"Yeah, it's that way sometimes. So how did you get the scar?"

"Ah…the scar. Sheila really did do it. Said I was too pretty."

He chuckled again. Loud and honest. I couldn't help it. I chuckled back. He seemed genuine and I was high and barefoot and away from San Francisco.

"No, well, yes. She did do it. But not to dampen my knock-'em-dead good looks." To illustrate this, Victor looked over at me, stuck his tongue out, and crossed his eyes. His focus then went back to the road and his story.

"We had been out having margaritas in a Chic-Chi's, 'bout five years ago. Damn good things, margaritas. But you gotta look out for those puppies. When we got home, she told me I had to take out the trash. I told her I had done one better: I married it. She slapped me. I thought about slapping her. Didn't. But I called her something I'll probably never call another woman again. A drunk angry one, anyway."

"What's that?"

"Cunt."

"Oh. Yeah, I guess —"

"Next thing I know…BAM! No, more like…CRASH! And I was out."

"What —"

"She hit me with the closest thing she could find: a lamp. Big old ugly blue ceramic thing we'd found at a secondhand shop. Crash! Right into the side of my face. That's one way to get rid of old things you don't want."

"What? You getting rid of your wife or her of you?" I laughed nervously.

"Oh, neither. The lamp. It was butt-ugly. I got my

face stitched up. She felt bad and then said she was sorry. And we went on as before for a couple years…like two more. Well, no, not everything was the same. I stayed away from lamps when she was mad. And we cut down on the margaritas. But other than that it was the same. Until she got tired of me ignoring her and took off like I said before."

"Uh. Sorry."

"I'm not."

"But why did you stay with her?"

"Honestly?"

"Am I being too nosy, Victor?"

"Oh, hell no, Tal. We might as well get to know each other. Honestly? I liked her. And she was a wildcat in bed. I'm a sucker for a good fuck. And I can forgive a lot."

The CD has ended and Victor presses play and starts it over.

We cross the Wisconsin River and the hills start to get a bit bigger, the trees a shade darker green and a bit denser, and the temperature cooler.

About 10 miles from the river, we take a turn off the main road and travel down a paved one-laner. Then another turn, this time onto an unpaved drive, and I start thinking of Ed Gein. Stop thinking about that! He's a nice guy! He's a client, not a scary psycho killer! God, I'm such a chicken. I start to laugh from the nerves.

"What's funny?"

"Oh, nothing. Just nerves."

"We're almost there."

Then the trees part a little and I see his house. It's huge, more like a lodge, like a ski lodge. I wonder if it was designed by Frank Lloyd Wright. Before I have time to ask Victor stops the truck, opens the door, and hops out.

"We're here. I'll get your bag. Follow me."

The sun is setting and with all the tall trees surrounding the house it is almost dark. It's beautiful and peaceful. A green cathedral.

I follow Victor through the front door into a large open living-room area with a fireplace and a bearskin rug, then immediately up some beautiful blond wood stairs to a nice cozy bedroom with a bath on the second floor.

"Go ahead and take a shower if you'd like. Or a nap. You look a bit traveled. I'll start dinner. We can eat in about an hour or so. Sound good?"

"Thanks, Victor."

He reaches up and strokes my neck. Rather intimately, like a lover or a father. His large warm paws feel good either way. He smiles and leaves, closing the door behind him.

\*\*\*

I take a long hot shower. I soap my swollen dick and balls with extra attention. I'm horny as hell and really want to cum but decide to wait in case there's any adventure ahead for this evening. I dry off, throw on my jeans and a fresh baby blue t-shirt with a gold sparkly PRINCESS decal, then head downstairs.

I find Victor in a huge kitchen at the back of the house. A long window lines the entire length of the kitchen, overlooking what looks to be a small garden area now in complete darkness. A long wooden table is laid out with bowls full of chopped food, enough ingredients for a feast.

Victor is at the stove frying tortillas one by one. He's wearing a large bib that says *Kiss the Cook*, so I do. On his cheek. Rubbing my hands up his sides. He brings the warm greasy tortillas over to the table and starts rolling them with the ingredients: meats and cheeses, cilantro, onions, nuts, dried fruits, and chiles.

"Can I help?"

"Oh no. Thanks. You hungry? I enjoy cooking for hungry men."

I sit down so he can't see the return of the boner. For some reason I'm feeling shy around him. He's so sexy. I decide I really want him to want me for more than modeling. I could use three weeks of good sex with a Daddy like him, but I'll play it cool and see if he makes the first move.

"Yes, very."

"Do you eat meat?"

"No, not often. Occasionally chicken."

"Good! I'm glad I did some. One of my own."

I tilt my head and give him a look that says "What?"

"One of my chickens. I raise them."

I was going to ask where since I didn't see any on the way in, but just say, "Oh."

"But no red meat, huh?"

"No."

Victor gives me that wicked smile and says, "Too bad. Jesus is partial to buffalo. And I must say I do make a mean buffalo enchilada! Well, I'll just make some for Jesus and me then."

Jesus? Buffalo? What? Is he kidding?

"Jesus?"

"Tal, this is Jesus. Jesus, Talvin."

Jesus is a little bulldog who has just come into the kitchen as if on cue. He jumps up and takes a seat in the chair at the head of the table, smugly looking at me as if he knows everything about me, and isn't real pleased. I get up and walk over to him to pet his head, then his back. He growls at me.

"Jesus, mind your manners. Play nice. Tal is a guest."

Victor finishes wrapping piles of tortillas stuffed with the different meats, cheeses, vegetables, and spices. He then covers them with a thick red brown sauce, homemade mole he says, and sets them in the huge oven to bake.

After about twenty minutes of watching Victor do his magic, we have cleaned the table off from the preparation and have it reset with food: meat and cheese enchiladas, spicy vegetable tamales, fried potatoes, rice and beans, fresh melons and berries, and a dark Mexican beer in huge chilled mugs.

Jesus keeps his seat at the head of the table and Victor and I sit on either side. A plate is filled with the "buffalo" enchiladas without the mole sauce for Jesus, and he stands with his front paws on the table and eats.

Victor and I take a bit of everything else. The combination of aromas and tastes is amazing. It's the best meal I've had in ages and I fight the urge to wolf it down. We eat slowly; savoring each and every one of the treats he has created, while continuing our conversation.

"Victor, not that I'm complaining about the work...but why do you want a live model instead of working from a picture?"

"I get inspiration from beauty. I have painted from memory, and even some from pictures. I've used you before."

I blush. "What, you mean from my films?"

"Well, I do love your work. And I have watched them over and over. Even had to buy a second copy of *The Prince and the Pounder*. But no. That layout in that magazine you did. What was it—"

"*Plugged Magazine*?"

"Yes. That one. I used it for inspiration in several canvases last year."

He has to be gay. That magazine is hardcore. And the feature was all shots of my ass getting, you know, "plugged."

Jesus announces he is done, with both dinner and our conversation. He belches, jumps down from his chair, and leaves the room.

"You know I didn't even get paid for that spread? Those were all stills from an early film I did with the studio. And the contract gives them complete control of use. It sucks."

"Yes, that does suck." Again with the smile. It almost winks by itself.

Please, Daddy, tell me that you want me.

I watch Victor eat. I'm in heaven. He eats each mouthful as if it is the best he's ever had. Like each bite is an orgasm. I wonder what it would be like to be devoured by him, what his face would look like while he sucked on my foot or fucked me.

"But I have found that my best work comes with the use of a live model. A chair may look nice, but you have to sit in it to know it's comfortable. An orange is pretty, but until you smell its scent and taste its juice you can't truly appreciate it, right?"

The OxyContin and the hot shower and the feast must have caught up with me. I'm feeling giddy and a bit confused. Is this a come-on? Should I just get up and pull off my way too tight jeans to get him started?

"Sorry. I sound cold. I've made you an object."

"That's okay. I've made most of my money the past couple years being an object."

"Do you want coffee, Tal?"

"No, thanks. How about another beer?"

Victor stands, grabs another Negro Modela from the fridge and pours it in my mug. He then grabs a few plates and stacks them in the sink.

I stand up as well and say, "Here, let me help."

I think about walking to him and slipping my hand in under his shirt and caressing his hairy chest and stomach. I bet he has large nipples. I imagine taking first one, then the other nipple into my mouth and sucking. Would he then force me down onto my knees and my head onto his cock? What would it look like?

I want to know how his balls taste.

"No. Sit. Relax. I can get them in the morning."

I sit. "It's beautiful here, Victor."

"Yes, it is."

"Were you born here?"

"No. No. I was born in Florida. Sarasota. That's where I met Sheila. Then we moved to Chicago. We bought this land when her dad died. We both thought it would do us good to get away from the city and all the noise, so we moved up here. I still think it's good. Bought her half from her when we split. I love it. It doesn't get much better than this: privacy and space, clean, no noise, no pollution. Room enough for friends to come and stay for as long as they want when they need to escape."

"Was this house built by Frank Lloyd Wright?"

"No, but there are a few of his houses in the area. It does look like one of his. We can explore some of them this week if you'd like. It won't be all work." He flashes me his teeth and my hard-on is starting to be painful.

"I'd like." I decide I might have to be obvious and let him know how much I want him. Just standing up should be the most obvious way right now, with the way my dick is acting.

"Ready to work?"

Slap! I hadn't expected to hear that.

"I, uh…"

I'm tired. And full. And really horny! But I am comfortable and kinda high and totally at ease with him, so why not. He's paying the tab.

"You can bring your beer. Let's go upstairs."

"Sure. Why not."

The third floor is gutted into one large open workspace with rafters and angled dark-wood walls. There are only two windows, one at each end of the space. New lighting has been fitted into the ceiling the entire length.

There is a low king-sized bed in the middle made up with white sheets. Next to the bed is a black pedestal with a large silver bowl full of oranges, grapefruits, and limes.

To one side is an oversized wood easel with a blank stretched canvas. A long table much like the one in the kitchen is piled with bottles of liquid, tubes of paint, brushes, knives and spatulas. He must mix the paints directly onto the table because it has mounds and mounds of paint in every color in varying states of drying.

The other side of the room is bare. Except for a chair and a large sling attached to the ceiling. My dick takes notice of the sling.

"You can put your clothes on the chair."

I strip with my back half-turned to him, somewhat self-conscious of my hard dick. This, of course, is silly since he has seen my work, but I'm feeling a tad shy. Like a teenager. My heart is beating much faster than normal. I place my jeans and t-shirt on the chair then turn around.

He has also stripped and has stuffed his clothes under the table. I guess I had no reason to feel worried about my boner since he is wearing a pretty impressive one himself. A soft coat of mostly white hair covers his entire torso down to his very long upturned cock and weighty balls.

Jesus has joined us and is sitting next to him on the floor at his feet.

"I work best naked. Is that okay, Tal?"

I smile and say, "Yes, sir! More than okay. Where do you want me?"

"On the bed…to start."

I lie on my back on the bed with my porn-star feet aimed right at his canvas, then give him my best angle, spreading my legs just a little to show my aching balls and ready hole, and grab my dick in my fist.

"Good?"

"Great! Beautiful! Such beauty!"

He grabs one of the bottles from his worktable, slowly walks to the bed, and hands it to me.

"What's this?"

"Lube."

I take the bottle from his hand, his cock just inches from my face. I close my eyes for a second to enjoy the wave of desire that has overtaken me. I lick my lips and open my eyes, hoping to take his cock into my mouth and taste him. But he has moved back to the foot of the bed, watching.

Not wanting to show my disappointment too much, I uncork the bottle and pour a generous amount of the sweet smelling oil onto my chest, then down to my dick and balls. I place the bottle on the floor next to the bed, then slick my entire torso, giving him a show, enjoying both the sensation of the oil and the excitement that Victor obviously feels watching me do so.

His face is totally focused on me, eyes drilling straight into mine. Even though I'm used to having sex for an audience I could cum at any moment. I lift my knees and spread my legs farther apart rubbing the oil down over my smooth shaved asshole, then inserting my middle finger partway in. Victor starts stroking his cock, his big hairy balls flopping up and down with each beat.

"Victor, you've got me so turned on I could cum right—"

"Mmmm…how nice! But try and hold off for a bit yet. Here…" He crawls onto the end of the bed, kneels, and lifts my left leg, supporting it with both arms so that my foot is in front of his face. "…Let me help you."

I slide my finger out of my asshole, then immediately all the way back in, "Uh…ooh…Vict—"

"Yes, mmm…" he says as he licks from my heel slowly up across my arch to my big toe, which he takes into his mouth, "Ahhhthhhppphhhfff."

"What?" I ask, sliding my finger free of my clenching asshole and gripping my dick with both fists.

He swirls his tongue around my toe, then pulls it free. "Your foot is beautiful. Hand me the lube, eh?"

I lean over backwards, grab the bottle and give it to Victor. He sets my leg down and pours a small amount into his palm, then onto his own cock, then sets the bottle on the floor.

Jesus is sleeping and I can hear him snoring.

Victor bends over my right foot and rubs the oil on it, massaging my toes, spreading them apart and sending jolts of electricity throughout my body. He then positions his beautiful large body over my foot and squats, quickly swallowing my big toe and part of another into his asshole.

"AAH!" he lets out as it slides in.

Victor gives me a show this time. He rides my foot like a pro, his hole now full of all my toes and the top third of my foot. His cock is swollen and dripping pre-cum and bobbing up and down. I match his rhythm, pulling my oiled hand up and down my dick, my cum starting to build to a point where I won't be able to stop.

"Victor, I'm gonna have to cum!"

"Yes, my lovely Prince. Go ahead, jerk off. Cum! I will too!" With this, he stops moving on my foot and just watches me. His ass is clenching tightly around my toes and the ball of my foot. He pushes himself down. I feel pressure then his asshole slowly swallows another couple inches. He now has the top half of my size-14 foot up his ass.

"Finger your asshole for me, Prince, now, and let me see you shoot!"

I lift my other leg up so I can reach and so he can see, then slide my index and middle fingers swiftly into my slick hole. I cum instantly — from the sensation in my ass and my dick and my foot and from the amazing view of my foot up his ass — my spunk shooting up onto my chest and belly in giant spurts.

"AAAAAAAAHHHHHHHHHHHHHHH…" I scream out.

"NNNNGGGGHHHHHHHHHHHHHHH…" Victor screams back as his asshole grips my foot, then pumps tightly around it over and over as his cum sprays out onto my legs and the bed.

Jesus wakes up and starts barking at us fiercely from the foot of the bed and Victor silences him with a soft, "Shhhh, not now, quiet," over his shoulder.

Victor lifts his bulk up and off my foot, and then my great Daddy Claus starts slowly licking me clean, beginning with the foot that had moments ago been buried in his ass, up my leg where his spunk has landed, to my balls and dick and stomach and chest where mine is now cooling.

"Delicious," he whispers as the last of my cum is slurped clean.

He then lifts both of my legs up and over his great

mass, pressing my knees to my shoulders with his hands. I relax back onto the bed and stare up at the dark wood rafters while his tongue sloppily weaves circles around first one then the other nipple. I can feel his big hairy belly against the back of my legs and his still-hard cock rubbing against my asshole.

"You mind if we skip painting tonight?" he asks between laps of his tongue.

"Not at all…mmmahhhhh…no. What do you have in mind?"

"I'm still hard," he says, kissing his way up my neck and over my chin. He softly kisses my lips and whispers, "And I want to fuck you."

"Yeah?" I whisper back.

He gently tongues over my lips, then licks my right foot which is next to his face.

"Oh, yeah—"

"Yes," he says, then softly bites at my most sensitive body part, just under the ball, my arch.

"Ahhh—"

"Hard." And his cock slips into me in one quick thrust, then out halfway, and again "HARD!"

"AHHNGG—"

And he bites my arch. "HARD!"

"AAHHHEEE!"

"HARD!" And he bites again.

"AHHHHHH!"

"AND FAST!" And he slams into me once again fully, gripping my heel firmly in his teeth.

"GAHHHHHH!"

"HAHHHDDDLAHH?" he screams around my heel as he starts plowing my asshole hard and fast, pulling almost all the way out then using all of his weight to propel each slam back in.

"YES HARDER! AAAAAAHHHHEEEEE…"

\*\*\*

I wake with an extremely sore asshole, a slight headache, and surprisingly, a hard-on, to find a still-naked Victor at his easel painting. I must have fallen asleep soon after he finished giving me the best fuck of my life.

"Hey, Tal," he says.

"Hey," I respond, looking toward the dark window, "What time is it?"

"It's early yet, my Prince. I've been painting all night. You inspired me."

He smiles at me and my heart starts racing and I blush from my face all the way down to my toes. I realize that I might be falling in love with this man.

"How 'bout some breakfast before we start work again?" I ask.

# SPIT

The first time Dodie spit on me my gut reaction was to punch him.

Or maybe I'm remembering it from a far more butch frame of mind than I possibly could possess or should. Perhaps I wanted to just pull my head away in disgust. Or yell out: Nooooo! Or maybe push Dodie's hovering fuck-slickened body away in time.

It doesn't matter really. I didn't react that way. I didn't punch him. And I couldn't have, anyway. My arms were firmly tied to his bedposts. My head grasped tightly in his warm wide hands. My mouth was held open by his salty thumbs, just seconds before sucking first one then the other as if they were as delicious as his cock, which they were.

If I had managed to move my head to the side his glob of spit and phlegm still would have landed on my face. So I simply watched as the spit left his mouth to land on my outstretched tongue and lips after first taking a long slow stringy trip in between.

But maybe that wasn't the first time anyway.

Maybe that was earlier in the evening.

Or was that yesterday?

\*\*\*

I was leaving the Eagle. I hadn't actually been leaving but had just gone out back for a piss. My friends hadn't shown up yet and I had been downing beer. The bathroom was way too crowded and I didn't really want to join in on the party nor piss on the already wettened boy in the trough. So, I left and headed out to the lot behind the bar, a parking lot full of motorcycles lined up, past my baby, a glimmering new candy green Harley Low Rider that made my cock harden in pride and planted a solid grin on my face — despite the fact I had gotten it second-hand and cheap thanks to a friend of a friend's recent and unfortunate financial situation — to the end of the lineup of bikes.

There stood a tiny baby blue Vespa, conspicuous and shiny and out of place among all the real bikes. Maybe it was my sense of superiority because I was a real biker now at a real biker bar faced with such a sissy ride, or maybe it was the four Michelob Lights I'd quickly put away while waiting for my friends to show up, or both, I don't know. But I unzipped anyway, pulled out my half-hard cock, and, after a few strokes that could have quickly become a full-on jerk-off — maybe afterward, I might have thought, focusing on the tiny little-engined squirt of a sissy bike — I took aim and sprayed my beery piss all over the rear tire, the frame, and then seat of the Vespa.

I don't remember giggling, though I probably was as I marked my macho territory on this inferior bike, and therefore, biker. And I couldn't wait to go back inside to try and scope out which fag owned it and dared to pretend to be a real biker. Or that's what I remember thinking…before that biker found me.

"What in the fuck do you think you — and your skinny white ass — are doing?"

The last of the stream of piss dribbled down onto my beat-up black Doc Martens, not that this mattered. They'd seen much worse than a little piss in their time.

My fugue slowly cleared and I imagined what he might look like: small-framed, red hair maybe, and glasses. Definitely glasses. Converse tennis shoes, or maybe sandals. A bookworm, a student. That would explain it. A nerd on a Vespa. I might even have slowly stroked my half-stiff prick as I thought this. I shifted my head to glare over my shoulder, giving him my trademark butch-and-kinda-crooked-toothed smile, at this point not even bothering to do anything about my half-uncovered ass and fat cock still dribbling piss over his Vespa. I slowly turned—

"I said, what are you doing, you stupid drunk motherfucker?"

He was only a couple feet away. Dodie was easily several inches taller than my 5' 11" frame. And though he was clearly angry, his voice was calm, commanding. I was startled, and probably didn't appear as calm, caught with my dick out and a stupid smile on my face, clearly surprised by the vision that had caught me. How had I missed him in the bar? He was a sight. Built like a linebacker, Dodie was tall, dark, and amazingly handsome. A vision of flaming beauty. His deep brown skin shined as if oiled, most of it showing, covered only in a tiny pink baby-doll t-shirt that was cut off mid-belly, and the shortest and tightest white cutoffs I'd ever seen packed on a man.

At least a man his size.

One quick glimpse at the tight puckered belly button and then down the trail of fur to the pooch of a barely covered and what looked to be very fat cock and I surprisingly relinquished my alpha-maleness to him.

"I, uh—"

"You, uh, what? Thought you'd show off your big dick by way of messing up my transportation? I am so over you tired old butch white boys thinking you and your bikes make the man!" And with this, he gripped me by the back of my neck. "Look what you've done! Mm, mm, mm...you are going to take off that skanky cheap shirt right now and polish my bike…"

And I was on my knees, jeans still undone and barely covering me, my now extremely hard cock pointing to the sky, my naked pale ass cheeks glowing white with the moon's reflection.

"Then you're going to suck my cock. Then and only

then will we think about how you can try and make this rudeness up to me! What's you name?"

"Ke—eee!" His grip on my neck tightened to the point of pain.

"Key? What kind of asshole name is that for the man who'll soon be opening up each and every hole for this queen's pleasure?" And then he released me.

What's going on here? My cock was so hard it hurt. The leaking piss was now replaced by an urgent stream of pre-cum. I looked up into his big brown eyes and timidly said, "Kevin. My name's Kevin."

And somehow my shirt was off, his Vespa dried off as well as it could have been in the dark with a cheap polyester shirt, his spit all over my face, neck, and chest, and his very stiff—and yes it was very very thick—cock in my mouth.

And he laughed and laughed and laughed.

Or was that later in the evening?

***

Besides having my arms bound way too tightly to move much, Dodie had my legs pulled back, his strong palms now forcing my knees down onto my shoulders, feet straight up into the air, pointing to Jesus just as I'd done to other faggots many many times before, and his amazingly thick gorgeous cock forced all the way into my asshole.

He was fucking me like I've honestly never been fucked before—turning my insides into one big jumbled bunch of electric nerves. He fucked me hard, then harder, ramming in and out, in and out, each time hitting my—oh my God is that my prostate?—as it had never been hit before.

All negative reactions to the sight of his spit leaving his body en route to mine died away when I felt his cock harden even more inside me and I saw the light burn even brighter in his eyes.

Was this the first time he spit on me? Does it matter?

"You like that, huh, my little butch bottom?" he said with a wet sneer that was a dangerous mix of sexy and down right scary.

"Fuck...unh...fuck—"

"Yeah, bitch!" He pounded me faster and I liked it. Oh, yes, I liked it!

"I...unh...unh...unh..."

And he spit on me again.

\*\*\*

He made me follow him back into the bar after he was done with my attempts to make it up to him — stumbling along with my sore but still unfulfilled big pink cock tucked uncomfortably back into my jeans, my piss-wet shirt tucked into my back pocket, my chest and face a mess of his come and spit — to find my friends and let them know I wouldn't be spending the rest of the evening with them.

They still weren't there, and Dodie didn't intend to wait. Who knows what they would have thought? Maybe nothing. Or maybe they would have thought — assumed — I was leaving to fuck Dodie's fag ass all night long, though I doubt it since he was halfway out of the bar and I was running after him like a puppy. Real tops don't run after men like puppies. For some damned reason I didn't really care. I left with Dodie, or, right after Dodie, following him out of the bar, around back, and through the lot where he had first caught me wet-handed.

Good puppy!

Fuck, what was wrong with me?

Still not sure how such a big flaming queen like Dodie could top me, but knowing nonetheless that there was little else I wanted right now as much as that very pleasure, I obeyed Dodie when he made me leave my Low Rider in the lot and climb on the back of his Vespa, clinging to him like a virgin schoolgirl out for her first ride, my arms wrapped tight around his waist as if I feared I'd fly off, my face shoved into his back as if I was ashamed anyone would see me.

And they did. No one I knew — that I know of — but Dodie and I were quite the sight riding through town to his flat: a big flaming black fag with a killer smile and sparkling glitter mascara, skin barely covered by his baby-doll tee and daisy-dukes, and a slightly scared newborn butch bottom, pink skin a-flushing with humiliation as he hung on for life to the waist of his new top like he'd never been riding before.

Or maybe that's just my twisted memory of it.

Maybe it wasn't quite like that.

Maybe I enjoyed the ride: Dodie defiant and proud and beautiful on his flaming, sissy blue Vespa, making his way through the streets with a new butch boy-toy at his back, a boy-toy feeling somehow free and exhilarated.

Either way I was definitely excited.

I knew that Dodie was going to fuck my skinny white ass crazy.

And I knew that he knew that this was just what I wanted.

\*\*\*

"Fuck. You are the most beautiful piece of ass I've ever had. Come on, baby, show me how you come." And he shifted his shiny body back, my knees pushed back to either side of my head, his cock still lodged deep inside of me, and grabbed my aching cock in his grip.

Dodie had come twice already, once in my mouth and once up my ass. Just twice? Or was that three times? I'm pretty sure he shot all over me earlier — last night? — in the parking lot. So Dodie had come two or three times, but I hadn't been allowed to yet. And I really really wanted to, needed to, come.

"Mmmm…Dodie…"

"Damn, look at that cock, Kevin. That is one beautiful big pink cock."

"Ah…Dodie…I really want to come…"

"I've always heard that it was so. But now. Whoo! Ah-ha…now, I know it's true. The bigger the dick, the bigger the bottom!"

He smiled at his so-true joke and his eyes, his bright brown eyes, drilled into mine for just a second before focusing on my aching cock, then another great wad of his spit was released and my cock was wet and he was jerking me hard and fast and I was going to come and his cock felt so good inside me and "fuck me Dodie fuck me oh my god fuck me harder!" and he did fuck me harder and I swear I could feel his cock actually growing I could feel him coming again and again and "oh my god, Dodie, oh my god!" and I came and came and he came and we both laughed and laughed and laughed.

Or was that later?

\*\*\*

That next morning — or was it afternoon? It was sunny anyway. Dodie dropped me back at the Eagle's parking lot. I was tired and sore. Tired because we had been up all night. Sore because he had been up all night fucking me.

Hard. Then harder. Then again.

I had left my clothes at his flat. At his instruction, and with relatively little resistance, I was now wearing the white cutoffs he had been wearing the night before. No shirt. No boxers. My boots were also still at his flat. In their place I was wearing a pair of silly pool flip-flops, pink-and-yellow striped, with big daisies that fanned over the top of each hairy foot from their grip over each big hairy toe.

Did I feel like a big fag? Yes. Did it matter? Well, yes, it did matter, damn it! But there was a chance that Dodie wouldn't pick me up later like we had planned unless I did what he said.

And I did want more of him later.

Or was it already later?

"Go on, Kevin. Collect your big-man bike. I'll pick you up here at 8:00, hon."

My asshole burned, and I was naked but for his daisy-dukes and sandals that should only be worn by some tacky, old, leather-tanned, Miami Beach widow. What a mess I was. Sticky and stinky, and now dressed like a queen. It was enough to make me cry, but I honestly felt more like laughing at myself.

I slid off the back of Dodie's Vespa and leaned in to kiss his sweet mouth. "Thanks, Dod—"

"And leave last night's macho attitude at home, girl! Relax a little."

He gave me a passionate kiss, then slapped my ass and pointed me toward my Harley with a hearty laugh. And he laughed and laughed and laughed, and I laughed too until I realized why he was laughing.

Dodie pulled away, his tiny engine managing to spit up a cloud of gravel and dirt in his wake, his laughter still loud enough for me to hear as he sped away. The miniature desert storm subsided as I sat down on the sticky seat and let the bright sun warm my face, then I squinted down at my hairy white toes wiggling under the big plastic daisies.

Wouldn't you know it? Someone had peed all over my Low Rider and I didn't even have a shirt to clean it with.

And I laughed and laughed and laughed.

# COACH

In his trailer at 41 Lake Mermaid Place, a once-deluxe trailer cul-de-sac built snug up against a pond—now a mud hole—on the outskirts of Weeki Wachee, Florida, Jimmie Ray Kingburg is all snoozed out and dreaming. Sleeping late on a Saturday after a very long week. Well, not really late for him, it was only 11:00 am. He's all twisted up in his dirty sheets, sheets littered with Ritz Cracker crumbs and hound dog hair and cat litter, birdseed and dirt and gravel from his front "lawn," stiff at points from yesterday morning's cum and the cum from the morning before and the morning before that, naked but for a pair of very dirty tighty-whities riding up high into his none too clean asscrack, giving the already stained area a fresh coat of "racing stripe." They're riding up tight and his dream is of Mr. Jason, his high school soccer coach—his best friend Penny Joy Jason's dad—rubbing his wide callused fingers over Jimmie Ray's tender asshole.

Coach Jason rubs harder, running his rough fingers all along his crack, teasing his smelly, oily, and somewhat crusty hole, and Jimmie feels a thick finger slowly worm its way in.

"You like that, Jimmie? You want some coach cock? Damn, boy, you got some nice ass! You finally gonna let me have some that sweet stuff?"

And Jimmie does want it. He spreads his legs wider apart for his dream fuck. He wants Coach Jason to fuck him. Has always wanted him to fuck him. Since he first met him back when he and Penny Joy were in grade school together and he used to hang out every day after school until Mr. Jason came home from work, sat down in his favorite living-room chair, and kicked off his warm, worn, and very damp gym shoes. After a while, Jimmie started fetching Mr. Jason a beer as soon as he came home, and moving the gym shoes to the steps just as a way to get his hands on them. Then he could smell Mr. Jason's feet on his hands the entire night, long after he got kicked out and had to go to his own home for dinner. When he was older and got to high school, he joined the soccer team. Joined just to be closer to Coach. He never outgrew the fantasy, even now, many years after graduation, long after Coach Jason retired and Jimmie took over as coach, long after the old man kicked and Jimmy was older than the Coach of his dreams had been.

Coach Jason and he are alone and Jimmie's on his hands and knees on the wet locker room floor, just as he always wanted to be. And the older man's fingers are probing deeper and deeper into Jimmie's butthole.

And Jimmie's dick is as hard as a goalpost, precum spilling, balls pulled up tight. Painfully tight, or maybe it is just the way his underwear and sheets have wound themselves around his body as he slept. Jimmie always wakes up with a boner, but this morning's is extra fierce. And while in his dream, Coach Jason is fingering Jimmie's hole, in bed Jimmie's fat dick is poking out through the pee door and he starts jacking it with his fist.

Jimmie moans deeply, rubbing his dick with one hand while the other yanks the underwear even tighter against his hole. He groans, then farts, turns on his side, lifting a leg up into the air for his Coach, and his arm bangs against the bedside table, knocking over the half-empty Old Milwaukee and getting his Grammie's stuffed Moo-Moo wet. Not that it would hurt it none considering how stained it already was. His Grammie, many many years back when she was around, kept killin' her pets, not on purpose, she just didn't have no sense about what was right and what was wrong for animals to eat. When she killed a new little kitten given to her as a birthday present by feeding it chicken bones, Jimmie's mom finally said enough was enough and got Grammie a stuffed cat instead. Grammie didn't notice it was stuffed and still tried to feed it every day, and it was stained from two year's of food being smeared on the poor little critter's face. When she died, Jimmie kept it 'cause it made him think of her. He liked having something to remember her by. But then, Jimmie didn't throw much out. His trailer was piled high with everything from papers and magazines to boxes of crap like the little slivers of soap when they got too small to use and cardboard toilet paper and paper towel tubes that he knew he might need some day. Piled so high it seemed like there were trails from one end to the other of the trailer, all twenty-five feet of it.

It was small, just the right size for him he said, which would have been okay if it weren't for the fact that he shared it with three fat cats, Ulysses, Fritz, and The Beave, an old blind hound dog named Boner, who got the name 'cause he always had a little bit of red hound dog dick pokin' out, and two grumpy parrots both named Bird. And Jimmie wasn't the best housekeeper. In fact, Jimmie was a pig. Not lazy really, just a pig. Jimmie worked hard coaching the nasty little fucks at the high school, and he just didn't see much use in keeping things straight and tidy. It was just like he liked it. Comfortable. And you get used to the scent of cat pee after a while.

So while Grammie's stuffed cat now soaks up the beer, Mr. Jason probes on. One of the cats, Ulysses, is digging in the very-full kitchen sink, trying to find the source of the scent of day-old sausage pizza, or perhaps the half-full glass of milk from the day before yesterday, somewhere down in the bottom of the pile of dirty dishes, and is making enough noise to almost wake Jimmie up. Almost. Awake enough for him to grab his favorite pair of All Stars right by the bed, and throw one at the kitchen and Ulysses, conveniently located just eight feet away. He's on auto-drive, asleep still, when a whiff of sour sneaker reaches his nose. And he pulls the second smelly shoe to his face instead of throwing it after the other.

Jimmie now has one of his favorite All Stars, no longer white but a shade of brownish gray, worn down but not yet dead, almost as comfortable as bein' barefoot, tucked under face, the open insides smack up against his nose. And he's loving it, loving the smell, which in his dream isn't his sour old shoe, but Coach Jason's damp, aromatic socks. He's breathing deep of Mr. Jason's wet-socked feet, high on the scent of them and the locker room, high on the dream of Coach, his only constant fantasy.

Coach Jason, now only in a jock strap and socks, sits down on the splintered locker room bench and peels off one of his soiled athletic socks.

"Come here, Jimmie," his Coach says before stuffing the entire sock into Jimmie's open and willing mouth.

"Yeah, boy, suck those socks. Damn, you got me all horned up! Suck 'em good boy, and I'll give ya what you really want!" he continues, as he frees himself from the jock, his huge fat hairy dick bouncing free and making Jimmie whimper.

Jimmie pulls on his own throbbing dick, and tries to suck every bit of sweat and funk from Coach Jason's sock as he watches the big man wag his hardness in front of his face.

*ring, ring!…ring, ring!…*

"Jimmie, I think you want some of this, don't ya boy? You want to suck my big fat dick?"

*ring, ring!…*

"Or do you want some of this?" And Coach Jason bends over in front of him, the full force of the asshole's breath hitting him hard and making him suddenly very hungry…

*ring!…*

mmm…smells so good, so good…so hungry…

*ring!…*

Jimmie wakes, grabs the peanut-butter-and-ketchup-stained cell phone from the pile of dirty clothes at the foot of the bed, and screams, "What!"

Bird and Bird echo a shriek back at him, Ulysses jumps on the bed's corner and pees, and Jimmie's dream is fizzling out. Damn!

"What!"

"Jimmie, get up! Damn you lazy bastard, oversleeping again. Come on, wake up. Did you forget we was going? Shit. Get your lazy ass up. I'll be over in ten! And brush your teeth!"

Fuck! He forgot Penny Joy was taking him to the races today. His dick twitches angrily at him to get back to business.

Jimmie mumbles "mmrfflllater" and lets the phone drop back to the floor so he can finish what he started.

Conjuring the still-strong image of Penny Joy's once-young dad naked, sitting himself full on Jimmie's face, and the scent of too-old sneaker deep in his nose, Jimmie grabs the waistband of his tighty-whities and yanks them off.

He puts them quickly over his head, the damp "racing stripe" full over his nose, and grabs his angry fat dick. Just enough time to jerk-off good before she gets here, he thinks.

Mr. Jason grinds his ass down onto Jimmie's nose and mouth. Jimmie jerks his fist up and down over his pre-cum–slick dick, ready to shoot strong and high into the air. Boner lovingly licks Jimmie's foot, which is hanging off the edge of the bed. Fritz and The Beave start fighting, claws digging deep, sending tufts of fur balls and painful-sounding meows into the air, and Bird and Bird start shrieking again.

Jimmie's about ready and he reaches down with his free hand and slides his middle finger into his asshole in one swift thrust.

Coach Jason grabs each of his own asscheeks, opening himself wider for Jimmie's tongue. Boner continues to clean Jimmie's foot. Penny Joy is still bitching at him from the phone on the floor. Jimmie hungrily licks the "racing stripe," tasting himself but wanting and wishing it belonged to his best friend's dead dad. Jimmie wiggles the finger in his ass and cums, shooting strong and high into the air, like every morning, just like every single morning, just as Fritz and The Beave knock against the lamp's cord, pulling it off his bedside table in a crash, along with Grammie's soggy stuffed cat, which Ulysses attacks, quickly chewing the one remaining eye from its soiled face.

"Jimmie! Jimmie! What was that? You okay?"

"Yeah, fine!" He yells back at his old friend, as the fantasy starts to fade and the last few drops of cum are squeezed from his now-softening dick. "Come on over! I'll be ready in just a couple…"

He knows when she says ten minutes she'll be an hour.

Jimmie collects a puddle of cum from his chest with his hand and wipes it on the side of the bed. Boner wastes no time in cleaning it up. He rolls over onto his side, finds what looks to be a partially eaten baloney sandwich — only he doesn't eat baloney — staring at him and tosses it on the floor for Boner, or Ulysses, or Fritz, or The Beave. He farts and falls back asleep.

# LOLA

Her name was Lola. She was a showgirl. I met her at Le Club X on a Wednesday night. Showgirl Night. I could have sworn she was singing — she sounded just like Vikki Carr — to me and only me — and her eyes never left mine until the song faded out and the lights dimmed.

When all the other girls would finish their songs, they'd flutter through the crowd basically begging for attention with larger-than-life beauty queen waves of their perfectly manicured large hairy hands. They'd blow silent air kisses from their almost-smooth faces, and whisper deep "Thank you, sugar"s from their overly bright red lips to the biggest fan and possible date for the evening. I couldn't ever figure out why they took so much time and energy to look so tacky.

But not Lola. She came right up to me, offered her delicate long-fingered hand, introduced herself, and swept me off my feet. I never knew what hit me. I wasn't sure I deserved her attentions, but I was surely thankful.

\*\*\*

*Poppa always said you'll know true love when it happens. It'll hit you over the head hard and knock you flat on your ass, never to recover.*

\*\*\*

She wasn't like all the other girls. This was no act. It turned out she really was singing. This was what she really was. Real class act. The real McCoy. When the others were done with their evening, the makeup would come off and so would the persona. But Lola was always Lola. A perfect size 8, with tiny feet, and the voice of an angel. And real talent: Joey Heatherton–with-a-big-cock talent.

I never asked her where or when she got her beautiful tits. They were perfect: the size of large peaches, lovely handfuls with dark brown oversized nipples that I could grind my teeth on and suckle for hours. And I did. When I got started it was hard to stop. And she liked it; she'd scream out and call me honey and baby — things no one else ever had — until she'd finally have to pull my mouth free by grabbing my ears or hair and yanking herself away. She'd tell me nobody made her feel better, though sometimes I could tell I bit a little harder than she liked.

I never asked her why she stopped with just tits, or why she did so much coke. I didn't want to know. I'm glad she did though, stop with just the tits. As I said, she was perfect. Besides, she never asked me why I had a tattoo of Ted Bundy on my left arm, or when, how or why I came to have just one testicle. We loved each other exactly as we were. Simple as that.

\*\*\*

*Poppa always said to be thankful for what you got, son. Be happy with the hand God deals you.*

\*\*\*

Her cock was long and bent upwards when hard, much longer than you'd think for a girl her size...curving up and over her navel, and I could suck on it for hours too. I kidded her once about sucking herself, and I'll be damned if the nimble little minx didn't flip her legs back over her head and manage to get half of it down her throat. I asked her if she'd let me do her like that, but she said it wasn't exactly comfortable being bent up like a pretzel. But maybe, sometime, if I was a good boy.

***

*Poppa always said good boys get their just rewards, but he also said good guys finish last.*

***

Our lovemaking was everything it should be, and more. After sucking on her tits or her pretty cock, I would slide into her from behind, doggy-style. She'd coo at me while I plowed her ass long and slow, and when neither of us could take it anymore I'd lift her up flat against me, impaling her, and she'd grab her own tits. She'd call me her stud, tell me to give it to her, and I would. I'd grind into her more furiously, taking her cock in my hand and jerking until she'd cry out and shoot, causing her ass to grip me hard, and me to shoot strong, way deep into her gut.

I fell hard. I fell head-over-heels-in-deep-love hard. And so did she. Or so I thought.

She started dancing at a dank little nudie place called Gentleman's Palace on the weekends. She had to pay the rent she said; besides it's not so bad. Nobody would know she was packing and the pay's good. Her boss from Le Club had arranged it, telling her she could rack up some good dough. I told her okay, but that I wouldn't visit her while she was working, that it hurt too much to see her doing that. As I said, I never actually felt I deserved someone as fine as her, so I certainly couldn't tell her how to live her life. Besides, I worked doubles on the weekends.

***

*Poppa always said that you should give a girl respect,*

*put her on a pedestal and treat her like a queen, and she'd serve you like you're a king.*

\*\*\*

But I couldn't stay away. I paid my pal Virgil two twenties, and gave him a promise to return the favor, to take over my second shift one Saturday night. I snuck in the Palace — laying down another twenty for admission and a beer — and sat in the back row so she couldn't see me. I sat through two hours of mechanical bump-and-grind before Lola came on. The tears that formed in my eyes and dripped down my cheeks while she performed were as much from her beauty and talent as they were from the shame I felt for her and the pain it caused me as the men cheered her on. I decided then that even if it meant taking on extra shifts down at the plant, I wasn't going to let her do this anymore. She deserved better. I would take care of her, make her my queen.

When she was done collecting the loose bills from the stage and blowing kisses to the audience, she ran off. I followed her through the maze backstage only to find her leaving out the back emergency exit. Out the back exit in the arms of a big dumb thug. A big dumb thug named Gino. Her boss from Le Club X.

I followed them back to her apartment. I couldn't believe this was happening. My Lola and Gino! I loved her. She said she loved me. How could she do this to me?

\*\*\*

*Poppa always said that a fool is a fool is a fool.*

\*\*\*

I've made some mistakes in my life, maybe one of them was falling for a girl like Lola in the first place. I should have known that I couldn't keep her happy. I also knew that it was a mistake to go the Gentleman's Palace. But the biggest mistake was breaking down the door to her apartment that night in a jealous rage.

The second biggest mistake was not running right back out the moment I saw her kneeling in front of big dumb Gino, sucking his fat hairy cock for all it was worth.

His head was bent back in what can only be described as ecstasy—eyes closed and a big smile on his big dumb face—as he pumped his hips in time with her bobbing head. He had removed his jacket, but still had on his shirt and tie. His pants and boxers were bunched up at his ankles. Lola was doing her best to swallow his hairy hardness whole. Her dress was pulled up high around her kneeling frame. She had one delicate hand gripping his furry ass and the other wrapped around her own cock inside the Frederick's of Hollywood panties I had bought her.

\*\*\*

*Poppa always said that time is relative, seconds can last minutes and minutes last only a matter of seconds.*

\*\*\*

I took in all these details in those few seconds, but for one.

Tears burned down my face and my vision blurred long enough for me to miss the only detail that really mattered. Gino popped his fat cock from Lola's willing jaws and grabbed his gun from the shoulder holster he was wearing. While I was busy wiping away the snot and sadness from my nose, he shot me right between the eyes.

It all happened in slow motion. Lola's hands flew up in the air, her lips—still open from his cock's forceful administrations—now formed a comic book O of alarm. At the same instant the bullet shot from its cold metal cylinder, his cock erupted onto my Lola's sweet, now fear-struck, face. The bullet met its target just as she screamed my name and my head exploded, showering its ruined wet contents over Lola's prized collection of Snow Babies.

She really loved those cute little Snow Babies.

\*\*\*

*A fool is a fool is a fool.*

# COYOTES

## I.

I wake up. I've been sleeping I guess, though I don't remember falling off. I've been dreaming of running and something is chasing after me I can't control. We've been driving all night. I just wanted bad to get to Joshua Tree by dawn. And we have.

After we get to the park I drive about ten minutes, then pull off to the side of the road. There's no one around. Deserted. The temperature is cool, the air real still. Funny how a desert can get so cold at night. I want Tommy to see a coyote, so we sit side by side holding hands just waiting. He's tired, but I tell him to *wait, just wait quiet an' one'll show*. We zonk out, waiting.

Tommy's sleeping like the angel he is, crouched up against the door of the car. God, he's beautiful. I'm so lucky to find someone as fine as him who loves me. I lean into his body for warmth, and hear him moan my name. I close my sore eyes and drift off again.

\*\*\*

I wake with a stiff neck and have to pee something awful. After checking on Tommy to find him still sleeping, I walk off the side of the road into the brush. The sun is starting to rise. I'm in awe of this place and its beauty. I remember coming here as a child with my family while we were all still together. I've wanted to return ever since. I can't think of any sight better than the sun coming up through Joshua trees.

My sister and I took a cactus walk with my mom and dad, and looked at the tiny cactus babies that pop out and lay by themselves like those Tribbles from *Star Trek*, only spiny. *Tripples*, my little sister Bobbie called them. She kept trying to run off and my mom ended up putting her in the harness and leash for the rest of the trip so she wouldn't hurt herself. I thought it was kinda funny, my sister on a leash like a dog, but she didn't like it none. She stayed cranky and cried most of the time.

It was the year before they divorced, my parents and us. I was eight or nine, and my sister was four or so. It was the last time I can remember us all being together anywhere but at home. They separated soon enough after the trip. We had to stay with our dad, though I don't think either of us wanted to. I remember crying when mom left. Dad said she was going to live with another man. He had said, *It isn't no place for you kids*.

I shake off the pee, zip up, and head back to the car to wake Tommy since the sky's getting brighter. He's come all the way here with me, told me most of his troubles, confessed his love to me. I want him to see the sun rise with me, to see why we made this trip, or rather why I made it 'cause now I know he had other reasons.

I slide into the car and crawl on all fours to him. When my hands touch him, he grumbles and stretches his legs out. I decide to wake him up the best way I know. I unsnap his cutoffs, and with sleepy muscles he lifts himself up and lets me pull them down over his tanned legs to lay at the top of his sneakers. He smells good, like sunshine and boy. I rub my nose in his balls. *We're here, sleepyhead,* I say as I lick them and then wrap my lips around his growing cock and suck.

We watch the sun rise through the trees, then head out of the park into Twentynine Palms to find a motel for a shower and some more sleep.

\*\*\*

We first meet at The World, on a hot Wednesday evening. It's packed and the boys are acting like fools, dancing and drinking and pulling their shirts off and all. I don't dance too much and am just watching when my friend Mark sits down next to me and says, *Hey, Greg, this is Tommy-Boy. Go easy on him, Tommy, he's shy.* Just like that, then takes off onto the dance floor. I look over and there he was, prettiest face I'd ever seen — green eyes and freckles sprinkled all over his nose and cheeks — though he is young-looking. But he can't be all that young, I think. He got in.

He smiles at me and I smile back. He stands up and says, *Let's dance.* When I say *I don't da…* he shrugs and takes off. I want to talk to him more, but he never leaves the dance floor, even dancing by himself at times. I go home when the lights come up, a little drunk and alone, 'cause he's disappeared. Well, I almost always go home a little drunk and alone. I'm not too good at finding someone who likes me like that. Must be 'cause I can't dance.

Mark calls me a couple days later and says, *Hey, stud, guess who wants your number?* I think he's joking. I can't believe he even noticed me the way he carried on that night. Mark says, *He likes older men,* and laughs. Older men? I'm twenty-six, not that old. *How old's he?*

Tommy calls me the next day and says he has Tuesday off from work. He wants to hang out with me, that he likes my smile. I pick him up next to the high school that Tuesday morning. I can't pick him up at his house 'cause he still lives with his mom and doesn't *want her askin' any questions.* He leans back in the seat, slips off his sneakers and puts his bare feet up on the dashboard, just smiling. He has on a real tight white t-shirt and some short cut-offs. His legs are smooth and tanned. I'm hard just looking at him and he knows it.

We drive around for a while, then go back to my apartment to watch some TV. I flip on Merv Griffin and before I know it he's leaning over and kissing me with his big pretty lips and running his hands through my hair. We spend the entire day in my bed, and I gotta say I'm hooked from then on. I drive him back by the school at five 'cause he says he has to meet his sister. I kiss him hard, and he promises to call me that night. He does.

A couple days later I tell him on the phone, *I got some time off comin' up. You wanta take off an' come on a road trip? A vacation?* He says *sure* real quick, *as a matter of fact, I was thinkin' of gettin' away.* So a week later, after figuring out a route west, we take off in my car.

***

We are just past Richmond, Indiana, not forty-five minutes out of Dayton, when he tries to tell me the first time. He says, *Greg, got somethin' to tell you an' I don't want you gettin' mad. I'm not...* He won't finish what he is trying to tell me. Then he gets all silent. I'm not what? Well, you gotta know, I'm more than a little mad at first. Here I am falling for him, driving cross-country on what's supposed to be a vacation, and all he can do is cry. Jeez, I never met any guy like him. I keep driving and he eventually gets better, but he won't talk for a while. I don't know whether to stay mad, make him tell me what's wrong, or turn back around. I just drive on and listen to Glen Campbell sing on the radio.

By Indianapolis, he's crying again. He tells me he was sorry to lie to me for so long, but he loves me and doesn't want me to get all crazy and not see him no more. He loves me? My heart is bursting with a mix of fear, and something totally alien, a love so deep it hurts. I don't care what else he'll say.

We drive straight through to Kansas City, where we get a room in a Motel 9. I gotta tell you the truth, although I'm surprised by the news when he finally gets it out, I know I'm not gonna stop seeing him. He loves me and I love him too. I feel lucky, very lucky. I guess I'm not too surprised either. He says he's fifteen.

\*\*\*

By Denver, he's told me more. He's told me most of his life story actually. It's like I pulled a cork out and he couldn't stop. His dad had died before he was old enough to know him. His mom had raised him and his sister Robin alone. He calls his sister Bean 'cause *she's tall an' skinny like a string bean.*

Bean is older than him by a couple years and lives in a house with her two kids, just a few blocks away from him and his mom. He calls his mom The Countess. It's not just a nickname he calls her, he says. *She calls herself that.* She started a company called Countess Connie Cosmetics and after that she was Countess Connie, or just The Countess.

About two weeks before I met him at The World, he says he was at home skipping school with a friend. *A friend?* I say. *Yeah, just some dumb jock kid from school, an' we're foolin' around. Pretty hot for a horny jock though,* he says. *We're doin' it on The Countess' bed when the front door bangs.* Tommy panics, he tells me, and grabs all their clothes and jumps in the closet. But the jock freezes, just sits there waiting with only his shirt on and no pants. Right before she steps into the room, the kid pulls the cover up over himself and picks up the phone pretending he's talking on it.

*Well, The Countess acts cool for a couple minutes just starin' an' watchin' him sweat. Then she grabs the phone out of his hand an' says, where's my son, you slut! Then it gets real bad, her screamin' at him an' I thought she was gonna hit him! I pull my pants on in the closet an' storm out yellin' back at her. Just leave it alone, Countess!*

He says the kid just sits there staring back at her kinda like a deer caught in headlights.

*She yells, you think I want to kiss a man who's been suckin' cock? What's wrong with you, boy? I throw the jock his* pants an' he pulls them on under the covers. On my way out she yells, don't think you're welcome back here, young man. I don't want you around any of my men! Bad enough your sister turned out like she did. I'm not puttin' up with another!

So I leave an' don't go back. My sister goes home for me the next day an' gets some of my clothes. I'd been stayin' with her when I met you, but I can't stay with her forever. Bean's got her own problems. She's kinda fucked up. But you saved me now anyway.

We take turns driving after that. I let him drive more than me, enjoying the view and enjoying watching him get such a kick behind the wheel. He seems different somehow now that I know his story, happier, free. I know that I am his for good. We stop once more, this time somewhere in Arizona, but just sleep in the car. We stop at a couple truck stops along the way to wash and eat, but we are both on a mission to get to Joshua Tree as fast as we can.

I worry his mom might try to find him, but he says, *She won't even miss me.* I believe him.

\*\*\*

He comes running into the room and slams the door, waking me up. He jumps on the bed and flattens himself against me. I'm barely awake, but his persistent rubbing wakes me up enough to pull him to me and kiss his lips.

I grab his butt, squeezing him through the cutoffs. I can feel his hard-on and try to unzip him.

*Where you been?* I ask him as he sits up and pulls the sheet off me. He grabs my cock. *I got a surprise for ya*, he says and starts pumping me. I put my arm over his shoulder and try to pull him to me. He flinches as I grab the bandage wrapped around his upper arm.

*What happened*, I ask as I turn his face to mine and notice that his freckled nose is bloodied too. *I got in a little trouble, but it's nothin'. Some guy didn't like the way I look.*

COYOTES

His arm has a new tattoo. It says GREG in a big red heart. The bloody nose is from a soldier at the tattoo shop who saw what he was getting tattooed and called him a faggot. Tommy had said, *Yeah I am, you wanta suck my dick, soldier?* The guy had been waiting for him outside the shop.

*Let's get some food*, he says. I say, *Sure, Tommy, but love me first.* And he does.

\*\*\*

The map says it is a two-mile hike each way to the oasis. *You boys better cover up*, the lady park ranger tells us. I'm wearing a tank top, shorts, and my work boots, wanting to get some sun and catch up with Tommy's tan. He has on a t-shirt and the same cutoffs and sneakers he wears every day. *That sun'll get ya after about ten minutes, sunblock or not*, she says before giving us the eye and going over to a skinny woman in a poncho humming a song to herself queer-like and digging through the tourist books.

We take off and swing back to the motel to get long-sleeve shirts, but then decide we'll be okay without them. On the way back into the park he says, *It's my birthday, you know. I'm sixteen today. Take me to the oasis an' fuck me silly for my present.* My cock gets real hard instantly and I smile at him. He's serious.

I say, *Show me your ID, son, to prove you're old enough*, even though I feel I shouldn't be joking about his age. He just smiles back at me and winks. He's old enough.

We walk for about fifteen minutes, shirts off, and it's heaven. Hot as hell in the noon sun, but dry. I'm barely sweating as we climb the hills, curve after curve, being careful of the holes for snakes or worse, spiders. I guess I don't mind snakes too much, but spiders scare me, especially big ones like they have here.

He's walking about ten feet ahead of me and starts crying out. I run to him, afraid maybe he's hurt. The skin's bubbling on his arms, blisters actually popping out in front

**171**

of our eyes. I make him put his shirt on with his arms inside of it and we start laughing so hard we both fall down on the path forgetting all about the spiders and snakes.

It takes us about ten more minutes before we can start back from laughing so hard. He has to walk slowly without his arms for balance. I stop to take a pee and he starts talking about blisters on my cock, which makes us laugh even more. When we get back to the room, I rub aloe on his skin, then give him his birthday present, twice.

***

We go to dinner at Vino's Pizza. We're halfway through our pizza, starting on our second pitcher of beer when we hear, *I swear, Ben, if I ever get my hands on that boy an' that pervert man that brought him here, I'll kill 'em. I'm gettin' that boy some help, an' his man is going to prison!*

Tommy has turned ghost white and is sliding down in the booth. *Robin told me he said he was in love an' goin' to Joshua. Joshua Fuckin' Tree! In love. What does a fuckin' sixteen-year-old boy know about love? You know it was a man too. She didn't say so, but what girl would want a cocksucker for her man? What makes him think once that man gets what he wants, he'll keep him? Even perverts have some sense!*

I turn around to look, but can't see her through the white lattice wall with plastic ivy that separates our booth from theirs. *Go to the bathroom*, I whisper. *Hide in the stall till I come get ya.* My heart is about to jump from my chest and I can see Tommy's really scared.

*I'm tired, Countess. Let's go back to the hotel an' go for a swim. Me an' Little Ben's kind of wantin' some love too.* They walk out past me. All I can see is her backside, wide and bouncy, and big red hair. So this is The Countess, I think. And a very big guy with a flattop in a burgundy pants suit who must be Ben.

As soon as they're gone, I pay the check and fetch Tommy from the bathroom. We run to the car. He stays in it, while I pack up our clothes in the room. We spend the evening laying on the car hood in the desert watching the stars and looking for coyotes, since it's our last night in Joshua Tree. I know we should leave, but I have to see one. Maybe it would make things clearer. I don't know.

*What are we gonna do now, Greg?* he says as he lays in my arms and watches the stars. *Wow, the sky's so big out here. You ain't gonna leave me now that you've gotten what you want, are you?* I don't have an answer for him.

Have I gotten what I want? I'm in California with a man who loves me, who has my name tattooed on his body in a heart, and he's just barely sixteen. His mother, The Countess, is somewhere in one of the surrounding towns in search of us, with some big guy named Ben in a burgundy pants suit. I don't know whether to laugh or cry.

But I know the answer. I kiss his ear, smile, and whisper real soft, *I do have what I want, an' I'm not gonna leave you. What do you think of drivin' up north, maybe Washington, an' I can tell you my troubles?* His big green eyes say yes, and he runs his hands through my hair. I feel like my heart's gonna break.

I see the flashing lights coming down the road through the park, and realize what's really gonna happen. My heart is gonna break, and we're not gonna see any coyotes tonight. I lay back and rest my head on his chest. Through my tears I watch the stars with him.

## II.

Rita Mae has just found a coyote skull in one piece. She had been hiking through her favorite patch of hills when the heel of her Dingo boot caught on something hard and she fell down onto the dry desert dirt, skinning her right hand and knocking the wind out of her. Luckily the skull didn't break when she stepped on it. She picks it up, kisses it, and breaks into tears. Rita Mae collects skulls, and this is the best she has found yet. It's a sign. Mother won't deny her now, she thinks, as she drives full speed to the park ranger's office to show her lover, Doreen.

She rips through the desert as fast as her old truck will take her and pulls into the office's lot, still amazed at her luck. She grabs the skull, climbs out of the cab, and slams the door. Squinting, she looks up at the scorching sun, then pulls the poncho down over her right arm holding the skull, and enters.

Doreen is scolding some young bucks about the sun. Why do they come here for a tan? Rita Mae thinks. The desert is sacred, home to special spirits, to Mother. Intense. Hot. Beautiful. But not someplace to sun! Go to the beach!

She starts humming, then singing out loud, and then laughing at herself. She can't help it, today is the day that will turn things around for her and Doreen. She's absolutely giddy with happiness.

Rita Mae giggles, then starts singing aloud again. The boy and man both look at her and she pretends to browse through the brochures on native cacti.

Fools.

"That sun'll get you after about ten minutes, sunblock or not," Doreen says, then gives them a scowl and heads over to Rita Mae. "Hey babe, what brings out the song in you? You look happy!" She hugs her.

"This!" Rita Mae exclaims and throws back the poncho from her arm to proudly show off her new skull.

"Put that down, Rita! I don't want to have to explain why you collect those horrible things. What is that, another dog?"

"Well, Ranger Doreen, you won't have to explain nuttin' to those old ranger dicks soon. Stick with me girl, and you'll soon be fartin' through silk!"

Rita Mae blows her lover a mock kiss, and starts singing her song again as she walks back out into the noon sun and climbs into her truck.

\*\*\*

Rita Mae puts the coyote skull on the shelf with the others, right between the German shepherd and her favorite, the monkey. She strips down to her bare skin, and rubs the special oil over her face, arms, and legs. She lights all the candles with one long match, picks the coyote skull back up, and kneels in front of the mirror.

"Mother, I found your gift. Now I give you my body as one. Show me your power."

She places the skull carefully on the floor in front of her knees, and spreads them apart, then farther. The sight of her own body excites her and she strokes herself, building speed as she watches the reflection of herself, wide-open, and the skull.

Her vision blurs as she climaxes, then she sees a bright blinding light, and then a vision of the two boys from the Ranger office climbing in the sun. Their skin is blistering in the heat. Then the vision changes. She sees the one, the young one, yelling at some redheaded floozy, calling her bitch. "You got no right, no fucking right!" he shouts. The redheaded floozy slaps him.

It's all gone too soon, but Rita Mae smiles. She picks up the skull and kisses it. "Thank you, Mother. Thank you."

She gets up, puts on a robe, wipes her hands and brow on a towel, and blows out the candles. I think I'll skip making dinner tonight and take my girl out to eat, she tells herself, maybe pizza. She places the coyote skull back in its place of honor.

\*\*\*

Rita Mae takes Doreen to Vino's Pizza for dinner. She wants to celebrate. She tells her for the second time about how she found the coyote skull, and that it was fate. Mother had wanted her to find it.

"Rita Mae, you gotta cut this shit out, girl. You're scarin' me. You want some more wine? Honey..." she catches their waitress by her sleeve as she rushes by, "could you bring us another carafe of sangria?" Their waitress, Joan, at the moment her sleeve is grasped by Ranger Doreen, is on her way the bathroom to puke.

"Sure, Doreen, I'll get you your wine on my way back, sweetie."

Joan has been having an affair with the manager of Vino's Pizza for about two months now. The manager, Bill Jenkins, had told her one night, just as the two of them were closing up, that he and his wife, Millie, were having marital problems due to her bad back and chronic headaches. He broke down and started crying. She had a drink with him, then two. They started fooling around twice a week on the evenings they both worked late. Now he was telling her that he was going to leave Millie and he wanted her to be his wife if she would have him. Joan doesn't really believe him, and isn't really sure she wants to be the new Mrs. Jenkins.

About three weeks ago, Joan started getting worried when her period hadn't come. Last week, she began feeling sick to her stomach and throwing up a lot.

"Fuck, what am I going to do?" she says to herself as she figures out what is wrong and wipes the puke off the toilet seat. "I can't have a baby. Fuck. What do I want with a baby?"

Rita Mae looks up from her plate just as the redheaded floozy and some big side of beef in a bad pants suit walk by their booth. "That's her, Doreen!" she says a little too loud.

Doreen looks at her and says "What, that's her who?" The woman and man walk out the door and around the corner of the building.

"Her, the one in my vision today! The one yelling at the boy. The boy in yer office!" Without realizing it her hand starts rubbing at her crotch. She digs her fingers harder through the soft stretchy fabric, and keeps nodding her head in the direction of the door. "Ah...oh..." she can't stop her hand, she is going to climax, and the restaurant is disappearing.

Joan slams the pitcher of sweet wine down on the table harder than she'd really meant to, startling Doreen, who is totally confused and dazed from watching her lover Rita Mae fuck herself in the middle of the restaurant. "Here it is, girls," she says, winking at them before heading off toward the kitchen.

"Baby, I think you're a little too excited. Today was a long day. Maybe we should skip the wine and get you some air. Rita Mae? Rita?"

## III.

Ben Mankowitz is getting just what he needs and deserves after the long day. And Little Ben is getting the ride of his life. The Countess, his woman, is riding him hard, pumping up and down on him like she's riding a carousel pony.

"Oh yeah, Ben, fuck me, Daddy! Oh yeah, you're the best, Bennie, give it to me hard...oh!" She squeals and moans like he's splitting her open. Ben actually isn't giving anything to her; she's doing all the work. As usual. He loves it when she talks dirty.

He watches her gyrating above him. "Countess, you sure know how to make a guy feel good. I think Little Ben's gonna shoot soon. Call me some names again, sugar. Come on, baby..." he says and thrusts up as hard as his fat tired body and the position allow him.

"Ooh, Daddy, is Little Ben gonna fill me up? Come on, King, fuck The Countess hard! Oh, Bennie I'm..." A banshee's wail follows that is heard all the way down the hall of The Holiday Inn in Twentynine Palms, California.

Her squeal does the job. Ben Mankowitz grabs The Countess' big tits, farts, then ejaculates. It's the best orgasm he's had in years. "What's got into you, Countess? I'll have to bring you to the desert more often."

"I just thought you deserved a little extra lovin', Bennie, that's all. You know I love Little Ben, and you've been so good about helpin' me find Tommy, I just wanted to show you my appreciation." She lifts herself up and off

Ben's soft dick, and plops herself down on the bed next to him, carefully hiding the rolls on her tummy with her arm.

He knows why she's fucked him so hard all right. She does love his Little Ben, but she also wants to make sure he continues to help him search for her runaway son, the little faggot. She should know that after five years of him sticking around, he would help her. But being a woman in a man's world — and being alone all those years with the kids — has taught The Countess that she has special charms that work. Using her sex goes a long way with most men, including him.

She had asked him if he would fly to Los Angeles with her. Her daughter Robin had told her that the faggot was "in love" and had run off to the desert with a man. A man? He isn't really sure he wants them to find the boy, but he came with her, of course. A good way to get a little vacation as well, he'd thought, since he hadn't really been doing much, except feeling sorry for himself.

"Come here, Countess, gimme a little more sugar," he says to her as he watches her fussing with her hair in the mirror. "Give the hair a rest, Little Ben's feeling frisky again. This time, I'm gonna show you some appreciation." He wags his hard little dick at her, and she lays back and lets him do the work this time.

***

Connie was twenty-eight years old when he had met her. He had been thirty-eight. They had met for drinks, then dinner, a blind date set up by a mutual friend. She was charming, intelligent, a knockout. Big tits, big ass, big red hair. She was all he could think of after that.

She wouldn't let him fuck her that first night, but she did the second. Within a week, he was having dinner with her two brats, and within another week, he'd asked her to marry him. He was hooked.

"Marry me, Connie. I love you," he'd said after they'd put the kids to bed. "Marry me, and you'll make me the happiest man alive."

"Oh Ben, stop that now! You hardly know me, and besides I've got a company to run. Countess Connie Cosmetics won't run itself! I wouldn't make a very good wife, and you're hardly the Daddy type."

She had two kids: the girl, thirteen, and the little boy, ten. The girl, Robin, was tall and gangly, but pretty enough. The boy, Tommy, however, was a fruity little thing. Too smart, and he was always whining or crying, and had a habit of walking in on him and The Countess at the wrong times. Why'd he have to meet the woman of his dreams and she turns out to have two fucking kids?

\*\*\*

He didn't know what got into him sometimes. What was he thinking? He loved The Countess, it's just that those damn kids—that damn girl rather, because he chooses not to remember the incident with the boy—they made him do it.

It had only been twice, damn her. How could she have been stupid enough to get pregnant? And The Countess, what if she found out? He knew he was dead meat if she found out her newest grandbaby was actually his. Fuck, he was gonna be a daddy, and The Countess a third-time grandma.

Ben, you've made a big mess this time.

The Countess had been ignoring him for her business for a while. He'd been let go by General Motors after fifteen years and had been hanging around the house doing nothing but watching reruns since. The little cunt Robin wouldn't let up.

"I don't know what she sees in you, Ben. You're just a big, fat, redneck, shit-for-brains leech feedin' off my Mom!" she'd screamed at him when she and her two nigger babies had come over to raid the refrigerator.

He'd grabbed her, torn off her blouse, then had told her to put the brats to bed so he could fuck her skinny little hillbilly ass. She tried to scratch at his face, but he'd grabbed her flailing arms and threatened to beat up the little shits if she didn't. He fucked her on the couch, then she and the brats left. She didn't tell The Countess, and nothing happened, until the next time something happened.

That time he had gone to her house. He threatened to fuck her faggot brother again if she didn't let him, and well, the stupid bitch believed that if she did do him, he wouldn't try to. "Try to" was just a threat. He probably wouldn't ever try that again, as the little faggot had almost taken his balls off the first time.

So here he is in California, hopelessly still in love with The Countess. Her son is a no-good runaway in love with some pervert, and her daughter is going to have his baby. He pours himself another Scotch from his plastic travel bottle, thinking about the gun he's left at home and how easy it would be to use it to end the torment and pain he's feeling, thinking about how it would sound as he cocks the hammer and slides it into his mouth. Thinking about how scared he is of the future.

***

He and the Countess talked to the sheriff and his deputy earlier in the day and explained what the deal with her son was. They said it shouldn't be too hard to find the boys if they were anywhere in the vicinity. Real good guys, those two.

They were right. Shortly after their marathon sex, Ben and The Countess got a call from the sheriff. They'd found the little faggot and his lover man. They were being held at the jail in Twentynine Palms for the night.

Since The Countess had been told she wouldn't be able to see her boy until morning, Ben thought he'd take her for a drive through the desert to try to calm her.

Maybe, he thinks—The Countess crying next to him in the car—I can turn things around. He loves her so much, even if she does look like a raccoon right now. She acts tough, but look at her crying about that good-for-nothing faggot son of hers. She deserves better. She deserves better kids and maybe she deserves better than him. Maybe they should send the boy to a boarding school, maybe he can get another position with General Motors since things are picking up again, maybe she'll give in and marry him. Maybe the kid won't look like him. Maybe he should just taste the gun after all.

He's driving fast through the desert. It's a cool evening, so dark he can barely see the road. He's thinking of pulling over to hold her for a bit when he sees something run out in the road. He slams on the brakes and they screech to a halt.

"What's that, Bennie, a wolf?"

"No, Countess, I think that's a coyote. A fuckin' coyote that almost got himself run over."

The Countess dabs at her eyes with a damp Kleenex. The coyote stands staring at the car lights, frozen in the middle of the road, looking kind of like the way Ben feels.

Ben slams his foot on the gas pedal, and almost reaches it before it darts from the road and disappears. "Fucking mongrel," he mumbles as he continues on in the dark.

### IV.

Rita Mae's visions continue at an accelerated speed. Mother shows her everything. She has visions of Joan and the Vino's Pizza manager, and knows the exact moment the abortion happens. She has visions of the pharmacist and his wife fighting over their love life while she's shopping, visions of the deputy sheriff, Rick, beating up a drunk in the single jail cell, while she's lying in bed, and visions of just about everyone in their little town. She soon forgets about the man, the boy, and the redheaded floozy.

She stops having to rub her special oil on each time

she speaks to Mother, or light the candles, and in time she controls her public masturbation after her lover Doreen threatens not to acknowledge her if she doesn't. But Rita Mae does continue to stroke herself in front of the mirror at home when she wants to be closer to Mother.

Rita Mae has always been the object of discussion with the locals. She has never backed down from saying what is on her mind, and her love of the poncho and the peculiar hobby of collecting skulls fuels the talk. But now people have started whispering about her knowing stares, her "fits" where she looks like she is going to start speaking in tongues. It's as if she knows secrets by simply looking at someone, which she does. Rita Mae is beginning to be known as "that crazy lady" by the children, and "that witch" by the old ladies.

Mother now freely speaks to her whenever she wants. Rita Mae feels privileged by this and listens attentively, which explains her rolled-up eyes and whispering at inappropriate times. But Mother's starting to tell her things she doesn't want to hear, and sometimes doesn't understand. Rita Mae is starting to get scared by Mother's voice.

***

One day, Rita Mae decides it's time to rekindle her romance. She plans a nice dinner for her lover, Doreen, to be followed by a little weed, and then some slow loving. It's been weeks since she and Doreen have fucked. Actually, it's been since she stopped rubbing herself in public to bring on the visions. Mother's told her to save it for special moments with just her, and Rita Mae has obeyed. But she loves her Doreen and knows that although Doreen has been real patient so far, she has been waiting long enough for the love to return.

Mother has another idea.

Mother tells her that afternoon to kill her lover Doreen, that she hasn't brought Mother any new gifts. She's demanding a new skull, Doreen's. Mother is going to leave her if she doesn't. Rita Mae is scared, and starts hitting her head to make Mother stop talking. She swallows a whole bottle of aspirin, and then a whole bottle of tequila.

Mother doesn't stop talking.

Soon after dusk, when Doreen comes home, she finds Rita Mae curled up on the bed shaking with a hunting knife clutched in her hand. Her face is all bruised. She won't speak, and Doreen can't get her to give her the knife.

Doreen sits on the edge of the bed crying. "Rita Mae, darlin', please let me help you. I love you, babe. What can I do? I love you! Rita Mae? Rita!"

Rita Mae jumps off the bed, pushes Doreen down hard, and runs out into the desert screaming, wearing nothing but her Dingo boots with the knife still clutched in her hand.

Doreen searches for days in the desert for her lover, and then files a police report with the sheriff and his deputy, Rick. Though sympathetic to the park ranger, they say they can't help. They can't get involved in a lover's quarrel. She will come back on her own, if she wants to.

She doesn't. Doreen never finds Rita Mae, or hears from her. Months later, she packs up the skulls and candles and puts them out with the trash.

## V.

You smile at me and wink. I look into your big green eyes as you say, *I love you somethin' fierce, baby.* Tears fall down my cheeks as I pull you close to me and kiss your lips.

Your skin is so pretty. Smooth. Freckled. I rub my hands up and down your naked body, massaging your muscles. It's been two years since we touched. I've thought of you nonstop during the time we've been separated, even when I've been had by other men. I've missed you so much.

I press my face against your skin and breathe in your scent, the smell I've missed so much, soft and a little sweet, like a baby. I kiss your legs, your butt, your back, your arm where my name is tattooed, your neck. I bury my face in your hair and lay flat against your body, squeezing you tight. You whisper my name again, and wipe away my tears with your fingers.

You look the same. The same as that last time I saw you, at the police station in Twentynine Palms. The morning after our night in the desert. I caught just a glimpse of you through the open door as you were led away by your mom, The Countess. The Countess! It makes me laugh just to think of her name…The Fuckin' Countess! The reason we've been separated. The reason I spent two years in prison. You turned around and saw me sitting there and mouthed those three words, then they slammed the door shut and told me I was in some big trouble. That's when I broke down and told them the whole story.

It breaks my heart to know you had to spend these two years with her. I've been in a cell, but you've had your own hard times to deal with, I'm sure. I'm so grateful to know you still want me. I'm so lucky I made it out alive. *I love you too, Tommy*, I whisper in your ear. *I love you, too.* The tears start again and sting my cheeks as they fall. I pull your body to mine and feel your hard cock press against me. I want to show you my love and wrap my arms tight around you.

\*\*\*

I wake abruptly when my bed is kicked hard. I jump upright, and you're gone. I find myself still caged. You were only a dream. Only a dream. The same dream I have every time I sleep. My heart is pumping madly as Digger, my roommate for the two months I've been here, strokes his stiff dick through the prison work pants and shushes me with a dirty finger to his mouth.

*Wake up, sleepin' beauty. I'm feelin' ready for some of your special lovin'. Were you dreamin' of me?*

I do what I have to do to survive, and today that means servicing Digger whenever he asks me to. I learned fast that I had a choice between letting Digger fuck me when he wanted, or Digger letting the rest of them fuck me. I chose him. They can be kinda hard on someone like me: convicted of a sex crime, 'specially if it's with a boy.

I'm always thinking of you, hoping my dreams will come true and that we'll be together again once I've done my time. It'll be worth it to have you in my arms again. I guess I'm lucky, in a way. Digger's not that mean compared to some of the guys in here.

You and I can finish our trip we started. Only this time, there won't be anybody hounding us. You'll be legal, and you'll be mine for good. We can go back to the desert. I still want you to see a coyote.

*I love you too, Tommy*, I think as Digger pounds against the back of my throat with his cock and the tears burn down my cheeks.

*I love you too.*

Twenty-two months to go, and we're free.

# GRAVITY

It starts with a kiss: one tender, soft kiss. We're parked out by the Henderson's old place; you know, by that house out on AA that has the billboard in the front yard, big enough for the cars traveling south on the interstate to see. ASK JESUS TO MAKE HELEN WELL. Only nobody knows who Helen is, or was.

Coal and I've just got off of work. We closed down the Dixie Queen together. It's summer: hot and boring. Just out of school, nothing going on, nothing much to look forward to but a cold beer. We drive to my house and I grab a couple six-packs of Bud from the fridge and motor down to AA where we can watch the lights of the interstate as cars drive past on their way somewhere else.

There's a bit of a breeze, and us just shooting the shit together in his beat-up rusted tan Camaro. Coal and I always have gotten along well in school, but never talked much other than locker room lies. Then this old sappy song comes on the radio...

"...God, I miss the girl..."

and he's babbling like a baby. Crying and saying how he doesn't understand how Deb could hurt him like she did. Deb is his girlfriend.

"Shit, Coal. I'm sorry, man. Don't cry, shit."

And I take him in my arms. It's okay; he's hurting. I take him in my arms, and squeeze. He lets me. I squeeze his strong body to mine, hoping I can make him stop hurting. Before I know I'm doing it, my hands take his sweet face and pull it to mine. I kiss a tear that's slowly weeping down his cheek, then his eye. I gently run my tongue over his lips, then between his bright white teeth, surprised at my sudden aroused state. It's like my chest is supporting a great weight, like the witches in old New England who were tortured by being laid down and having stone after stone placed on them. Only it feels good. Real good and I'm hard. I'm touching Coal and I'm hard.

He looks into my eyes. He kisses back. We kiss: one tender, soft kiss. My life is suddenly very different.

\*\*\*

"Gravity, motherfucker! Gravity!" he yells as he bounces up from the bed on his strong legs and taps his palms on the ceiling. "Gravity."

We're so looped. A double feature at the Zucker Drive-In, two-tabs-of-blotter-acid-each-and-a-bottle-of-spiced-rum looped. Coal had said he wanted to fuck me in a hotel, and I'd wanted him to, so we drove to Tipp City and while he hid in the car, giggling like an idiot, I got us a room.

"Come on, Vic...come on! Gravity!"

I'm watching him from the other bed as he does his trampoline jumps, his fat cock bouncing up and slapping his brown tanned belly with every descent, his large heavy balls making thumping noises against his thighs. My vision is blurred; whether his leaps are slowed-down or speeded-up I can't tell; he's just a white blur of light and motion with a hard-on.

A hard-on I want to eat. I picture it on a bed of lettuce with a slice of Wonder and a couple fluorescent pickles.

It's a week since the kiss. He kissed me back, but then said he had to get home and drove like a bastard out of hell to get me back to my place, dropping me off and speeding away without a word about what had happened. I ran in the house, into the bathroom and jerked off, coming on the mirror above the sink after just five quick jerks of my fist.

Nothing was said until earlier today at work when he showed me the acid and asked if I wanted to see the monster pictures at the Zucker.

"Gravity!!!" and he's suddenly flying across the room at me, knocking me off the bed with a loud thump under his full weight. His hand grips my cock through my boxers and starts pumping, keeping time with his other hand wrapped around his own.

I'm laughing, uncontrolled and hard, the effect of the drug or the rum or him. My head bends down to the plate of cock, but first I flick away the pickles. I lick the bead of come off his piss slit, then wedge the head into my mouth. Not knowing what to do with the slice of Wonder and lettuce, I fling them across the room sending trails of color with them. His cockhead seems to be larger than my mouth, but somehow I manage to make it fit.

The stinky brown shag carpet burns as we twist and bend over and around each other, but I don't care. I am too enthralled with the taste of his body, the pinpricks of sensation along my skin, his deep musky scent, like the locker room at our old school, but better. I have already come once, in his mouth. But he hasn't stopped stroking me with his lips. I have my middle finger up his ass and he is fucking hard into my throat, his knees on either side of my head, balls flapping heavily against my eyes with each thrust. His ass swallows my finger, then two. I think of my arm up inside him and then he's pulsating, his cock expanding, contracting, pumping. My mind flashes greens, then blues, then bright white-silver. I think, Gravity, Coal, gravity. His fat cock finally shoots, and I know I love him. He pushes farther into me, down my throat. His come tastes like the pepperoni sausage we put on the mini-pizzas at the Queen, and I pull his thick red dick out with my hand and squeeze and it sprays my mouth and lips and tongue as I mouth "I Love You I Love You" and his ass squeezes my fingers tight and he screams, "Vic Oh Vic Oh!"

\*\*\*

For two weeks we meet every day. As best friends. As lovers. We explore each other's bodies, we talk, get high. I can't believe it, but I feel as if somebody really, finally, knows me. Nobody at work suspects the truth that two of Piqua's recently graduated have joined the ranks of the faggot brotherhood. That the king jock from Piqua High, Coal, goes down on cock: mine.

We meet before work, after work, and on nights when we close the Queen alone, we suck and fondle and paw between customers. I let him fuck me. When he shot deep inside me the first time I heard him say it. He said, "I love you, Vic." Soft and sweet as anyone could possibly say it. He didn't know it, but I cried as his cock plowed hard into my ass before exploding again within minutes of the first.

He says that he wants to go away; get out of Ohio. Maybe Chicago. That we're good together. Who cares about what people would think? He doesn't. I don't anymore.

And then it ends. No kiss. No tender soft kiss, just cold, flat words through the phone wires. He calls me on the phone and severs my life force just as if he took his favorite hunting knife and slit deep into my throat.

"Why not, man? What happened? What the fuck happened?!"

"It's just over, Vic. Forget it!"

"Forget it? Coal, shit...I love you! I thought..."

"Shut up, you do not! Stop sounding like a fag, Vic! It's over!"

He hangs up.

It's over, just like that. I pull my cock out and roughly, angrily, grind as I think about what he's said. I wrap the phone cord tightly around my balls until they look like they'll burst; I start to cry. He said Deb was pregnant and wouldn't have an abortion. Somehow his dad found out and now Coal is getting married. Married! I feel like my life just ended. I want his soft lips on mine again. I thought...

I imagine his blade forcing its way into my throat and the pain it causes. I see Deb's face smiling as he kills me, my blood flowing freely, draining.

I come all over my sneakers just as the alarm sounds, not even realizing what the alarm means. I rub the spunk from my hands on my jeans and wander out the front door staring at the sky's dark green color. My dick is hanging out and I don't care. I walk out to the cornfield in a daze.

I am peeing on the old weathered scarecrow my dad and I put up when I was nine when I first hear it. Thunder? The wind whips the stream of pee on me and I fall down yanking my jeans off, not concerned with anyone seeing, just wanting to be free of them. I pull off my t-shirt and rub my hands over my chest and belly, yanking on my nipples as if I can pull them off. Nobody's around. There's never anyone around. I hate it here! I hate...it sounds like a train is headed right at me and a smile forms on my tear-stained face. It's a fucking tornado! Huge and black covering the entire horizon. Electricity sparkles around me and my body hair stands at attention. I watch it pick up Aunt Felice's house and devour it, then the barn across the field. I am awestruck and my cock juts out strong and stiff. Running isn't even an option. I raise my arms to the sky and think of what happened the past couple weeks with Coal. I picture his bright teeth when he smiled at me. My Coal, my love. Over. I have nothing; feel nothing. I ask Jesus to make me well—Fuck Helen! I am lifted from the ground violently; arms spread skyward like a rocket launching, my eardrums bursting from the overwhelming roar, and I fly into my new destiny.

Gravity, motherfucker, gravity.

Greg Wharton is an editor for two Web magazines: *SuspectThoughts.com* and *VelvetMafia.com*. He is also the editor of numerous anthologies including *The Best of the Best Meat Erotica*, *The Big Book of Erotic Ghost Stories*, *Law of Desire: Tales of Gay Male Lust and Obsession* (with Ian Philips), *The Love That Dare Not Speak Its Name: Essays on Queer Sexuality and Desire*, *Love Under Foot: An Erotic Celebration of Feet* (with M. Christian), and *Of the Flesh: Dangerous New Fiction*. He lives in San Francisco with a brilliant Lammy Award-winning gentleman sadist named Ian, a cat named Chloe, and a lot of books.